RACHEL DAVIS—her determination never to be poor again pushed her to the limits of decency. Nothing would stop her from getting what she always dreamed of.

STEVEN FRAME—his one mistake would cost him everything he held dear in his life. There was no turning back now. He had to make a new life for himself. Love wasn't everything, after all.

ALICE MATTHEWS—her belief in Steven was shattered, yet she could not harden her heart to him. Maybe she needed to stay away from Bay City so she could forget the past—the good memories, as well as the bad.

———————

Series Story Editor **Mary Ann Cooper** is America's foremost soap opera expert. She writes the nationally syndicated column *Speaking of Soaps*, is a major contributor to soap opera magazines, and has appeared as a guest on numerous radio and television talk shows.

Martha Winslow, author of *Love's Encore*, is a renowned novelist and television writer who currently resides in New York City.

Dear Friend,

Rachel's love for Steven Frame drove her to desperate acts. She would lie, cheat, or steal to win back his undying affection. Steve, however, only had eyes for the fair and lovely Alice. Theirs was a love that survived frequent separations, misunderstandings, and jealousies.

As we begin Book 4 of the *Soaps & Serials* paperbacks chronicling the rich history of ANOTHER WORLD, we see their love put to its greatest test. Rachel pulls out all the stops and stages her best scheme to keep Alice and Steven apart. Only this time, Rachel has an ally in her underhanded dealings. Little does she know that this "friend" will someday turn on her and conspire to destroy her happiness. Ah, but that's another book. . . . For now, we're left with the question of how long Rachel can keep Steven dancing to her tune. Can frail Alice hope to stand in the way of Rachel's dastardly plan? Read on and find out.

For Soaps & Serials Books,

Mary Ann Cooper

Mary Ann Cooper

P.S. If you missed *Soaps & Serials's* earlier novelizations of ANOTHER WORLD and can't find them in your local book source, please see the order form inserted in the back of this book.

ANOTHER WORLD

4
LOVE'S ENCORE

PIONEER COMMUNICATIONS NETWORK, INC.

Love's Encore

ANOTHER WORLD paperback novels are published and distributed by Pioneer Communications Network, Inc.

SOAPS & SERIALS™ is a trademark of Pioneer Communications Network, Inc.

ISBN: 0-916217-34-5

Printed in the United States of America

10 9 8 7 6 5 4 3 2 1

LOVE'S
ENCORE

Chapter One
New Lives, Old Lovers

A young woman hesitated on the first of a short flight of steps that led to one of those narrow Park Avenue terraces. The bright Indian summer sunshine glinted in her taffy-colored hair and lit up her pale Dresden-china-doll complexion. She knew New York well enough to realize that, though the few junipers and rhododendrons furnishing the terrace were no match for even one modest front yard of one modest home in Bay City, they bespoke money, and a great deal of it. Taking a deep breath, she pushed through the amber-tinted door.

The doorman rang her up, and she was met at the end of a long, plush-carpeted corridor by a tall, middle-aged woman, lean and nervous, who introduced herself as Louise Goddard.

"And you are Alice Talbot?" the woman continued primly.

Alice held out her hand and put on as gracious a smile as she could muster. "Yes, I am."

When Alice Matthews Frame left her husband, Steven,

she flew to New York City. She didn't plan to go to New York. She didn't plan to go anywhere. She was going *from*, fleeing her husband.

Some months earlier, after losing the baby she and Steven had looked forward so to having, after grieving over it, Alice had gone back to work as a registered nurse in Bay City's Memorial Hospital. On an otherwise unremarkable afternoon in September she was given a message to stop by her husband's office to pick him up on her way home from work. Once in the office, she heard sounds from his bachelor apartment, one flight up, an apartment he used now only to house out-of-town staff or to work in when he wanted to be undisturbed. Taking the private elevator up, stepping off into the dimly lighted foyer, Alice heard the sultry voice of Rachel Clark, her former sister-in-law and the mother of Steven's son, Jamie, conceived and born while Rachel was married to Alice's brother, Russ.

The apartment, too, was dimly lighted, and soft music was coming from the stereo system that took up one wall of the living room, but what Rachel was saying came clearly to Alice. "Why have you been so frightened of seeing me?" she was asking. "You set up the agreement about seeing Jamie so you wouldn't have to have any contact with me, but it wasn't for Alice's sake. It was for your own. Why can't you admit it? We have more in common than anyone knows. That day when Alice lost her baby and we were together, I felt closer to you than I've ever felt to another man."

Stunned, Alice turned and fled.

The day she had had the accident that led to the loss of her baby, she and Steven had been cleaning out a closet together when a phone call came for him—from one of his field men, he had said. He had to go meet him.

Only it hadn't been a field man. Alice now knew it had been Rachel.

Hurt and confused, Alice drove home—to the house out in the country that Steven had designed and built just for her. Her dream house, he had said. Now everything was a nightmare. Leaving her car in the circular driveway, she ran inside, called a cab, then hurried upstairs to pack a bag. If she stayed here, Steven would talk his way out of this latest betrayal of her, and she would let him do it, because—God help her—she loved him almost more than life itself. Her only salvation was to run from him, hide from him. Once on her own she could find some way to put him out of her mind and heart forever.

When she reached the airport, she found that the next flight out was for New York City. She took it.

Checking into a residential hotel there under the name Alice Talbot, she wrote a note to her parents saying:

Something so terrible happened tonight that I can't begin to tell you about it. I am leaving Steven. I don't know where to go, or what to do, but I cannot stay in Bay City with him there. Please don't worry. I'll write when I'm settled.   Love, Alice.

For the next two weeks she got through each day and night the way she had gotten through the days and nights following her miscarriage—with grit and determination. She began reading the want ads. If going back to work had helped her then, it would surely help her now.

One of the ads she responded to sought a governess. Within a few days after writing to the box number given she received a phone call from a woman requesting her to come for an interview.

* * *

Shaking hands with her, Mrs. Goddard led her into the living room, a large, sunny room furnished in yellow and cream chintz.

Sitting down in one of the cream-colored armchairs, Alice smiled again pleasantly. "You have a beautiful apartment, Mrs. Goddard."

Mrs. Goddard gave her a thin smile in return. "It's not my apartment, Miss Talbot. I'm only the housekeeper. The apartment belongs to Eliot Carrington. I assume you've heard of him."

Alice's mind raced. "Yes. I know the name, but can't— oh, yes. A newspaperman, isn't he?"

Mrs. Goddard nodded. "Yes. And, I might add, an internationally celebrated one."

Oh, dear, Alice thought. *He sounds dreadful. And why does this household want a governess?*

She was about to put her question into words when it was answered for her by the appearance of a boy who looked about nine or ten. He came over to her with a shy smile. "Hi. I'm Dennis. Are you my new governess?"

"I'd like to be," Alice said. "How old are you, Dennis?"

"Twelve." Measuring Alice's look of surprise, he shrugged. "You probably thought I was younger," he said, toeing the carpet. "Everybody always does. I have a heart problem. That's why I can't go to school like other kids."

"You must be very lonely—" Alice began sympathetically.

"You would have to help with his schooling," Mrs. Goddard interrupted. "A tutor comes days."

Alice nodded. "I see." Her heart went out to the boy, who looked so vulnerable and, yes, forlorn.

"So will you take the job?" Dennis prodded. He sounded a bit anxious, causing Alice to wonder how many governesses had preceded her and why they hadn't stayed. Was it their dissatisfaction with the job, or Mrs. Goddard's dissatisfaction with them?

"You have references, I assume," the housekeeper said briskly.

There was the stumbling point—and the reason she hadn't sought work as a nurse here in New York. No hospital would hire her without proof of her R.N. degree, and she couldn't supply that proof without using her real name. And once her identity was established it would be easy—or at least not overwhelmingly difficult—for Steven to track her down.

"Yes, I have references," she said, "but—well, may I meet Mr. Carrington?"

Alice could almost see the woman's hackles rising. "I don't see why that's necessary. Mr. Carrington trusts me to interview all the applicants—to screen them for him."

As if he didn't see why it was necessary either, Dennis slung his thumb in his pockets and slouched out of the room.

"Yes, I understand that," Alice said in the most reasonable tone of voice she could muster, "and I'm sorry to sound as if I'm trying to go over your head, but if I could just speak to him—to explain my circumstances."

Mrs. Goddard had been sitting opposite Alice on the long, overstuffed sofa. Now she stood up. "I'm sorry, Miss Talbot, but I'm afraid that isn't possible. Mr. Carrington is a very busy man—much too busy to have to concern himself with matters like this."

Following Mrs. Goddard's lead, Alice stood too, telling herself it was probably just as well. If Eliot Carrington were only half as stuffy as Mrs. Goddard, he'd be impossible to work for. She might as well look somewhere else. "I'm sorry, too," she said, "to have taken up your time for nothing, Mrs. Goddard."

She was following the housekeeper to the apartment door when she heard a masculine voice say, "Just a minute, please," and she looked up to see a man coming down the hall toward her with Dennis in tow. He was tall and lithe, with a long face and an aquiline nose, but his expression was friendly and open. He held out his hand as he approached her. "Miss Talbot?"

"Yes," Alice said, shaking hands with him.

"I understand you wanted to speak to me?"

"Yes. I thought I—well—" She turned to include Mrs. Goddard, I didn't mean to sound as if I was going over her head, but I—"

Mrs. Goddard cut her off. "If Mr. Carrington wishes to speak to you, Miss Talbot, I'm sure it's none of my affair. And now, if you'll excuse me." She turned and swept out of the room.

Father and son exchanged glances, then, to Alice, Eliot Carrington said with a broad gesture, "Why don't we go back to my study? We can talk there." He laid a hand on Dennis's shoulder. "Can you make yourself scarce, son?"

Dennis nodded. "Yeah, Dad."

The study was lined with book-crammed shelves. More books were piled on tables and on the floor, and the desk was a mass of papers. "Excuse the disarray," he said, showing her to a leather armchair, "but believe it or not, I know exactly where everything is."

Put at ease by Carrington's breezy manner, Alice settled into the comfortable old chair. Eliot Carrington wasn't the least bit stuffy. "I believe you," she said. "And I hope you can believe me when I tell you what I have to say."

He sat down behind his desk. "Go ahead."

Alice took a deep breath and plunged into her story. "I'm using the name Talbot because I've left my husband and I don't want him to know where I am. If he knows, he'll come after me."

Eliot Carrington studied her. "And you don't want that?"

She shook her head vigorously. "No."

"But you do have qualifications for the job here?"

"I would say so, yes."

The newspaperman rested his elbows on the desk top. "How much do you know about my son, Miss Talbot—or is it Mrs. Talbot?"

"No. Miss. And to answer your question, Mr. Carrington, all I know is what Dennis told me—that he has a heart problem—and I assume from his underdevelopment that it's a congenital defect of some kind."

His eyebrows went up. "You sound like a medical person."

She responded matter-of-factly, "I am a medical person. I'm a registered nurse."

"Then you're overqualified for the job here."

"Maybe so," Alice conceded, "but under the circumstances, it might be difficult for me to find work in a hospital. Mr. Carrington I've always liked working with children, and maybe, with my medical experience, I could help Dennis more than some other governess."

He pondered that a moment. "Maybe you could. And Dennis has more than a heart problem. He has some emotional ones as well." Eliot Carrington picked up a pencil from the desk and rolled it between fingers—long and lean like the rest of him. "My wife and I are separated, Miss Talbot. I have custody of Dennis—not because my

13

wife is an unfit mother. She's devoted to Dennis, and he is to her. But she doesn't have the time to give him. She lives abroad most of the time."

"I see," Alice said. She could also see from the picture half-turned to her on his desk that his wife was a stunning blonde, slim and elegant, who looked like a movie star. A rich, pampered movie star.

"She visits Dennis from time to time," he continued, "but as you'll see for yourself if you take the job, she generally manages to upset him when she does come."

Not knowing what to say to that, Alice said nothing.

"And, as you've already seen, Mrs. Goddard isn't the easiest person to get along with."

"That was partly my fault," Alice insisted. "As tactfully as I tried to put it, what I said had to be insulting to her. It's just that I don't want anybody to know my identity."

With a quizzical look Eliot Carrington asked. "Not even me?"

"I'm sorry, but yes. Not even you."

"Then I'm going to have to take you on faith, it seems."

Alice thought for a moment. "No. Not entirely. If you would let me dial the hospital I used to work for, and then put you on, if you'd ask for Dr. Stillwater—he's the head of cardiology there—he can vouch for my credentials."

This time Eliot Carrington was amused. "And how am I to ask about you if I don't know your name?"

Alice felt the blood rush into her face. "Oh, of course. How stupid of me. I'm not very good at this, am I?"

"If you're not very good at it, then you're undoubtedly telling me the truth. Is Alice your real name?"

"Yes."

"Does Dr. Stillwater know you well enough to recognize your voice?"

"Yes." She wasn't quite sure what he was getting at.

"Then ask for him and tell him what you want." Eliot pushed the phone toward her. "He can tell me you're what you say you are."

Alice let out a quick little sigh of relief. "Oh, right. I'm glad one of us is clever." She dialed the hospital, saying to the operator, "Dr. Stillwater, please," and when he came on the line she said, "Dr. Stillwater, it's Alice."

"Alice!" She could hear the surprise and concern in his voice. "What's happened to you? Are you all right?"

"Yes, I'm fine. I'm sorry I left the way I did, without giving notice or anything. But—well—I had to leave, Dr. Stillwater."

"Where are you?"

"I don't want to say, because I don't want Steven—I don't want anybody to know. But, Dr. Stillwater, I've applied for a job to take care of a twelve-year-old boy with a congenital heart defect. I'm with the father now, and I'd like him to know I'm a registered nurse, and able to do the job."

"Put the father on."

"I'm using—another name." Alice hesitated for a split second, "and I've explained to him why, but will you please not use my real name when you talk to him?"

"If you like, Alice. Put him on."

She handed the receiver to Dennis's father.

His end of the conversation consisted mostly of "yesses" and "I sees" and "I understands," but when he hung up he said, "Dr. Stillwater thinks very highly of you."

Alice felt her color rise again. "I think very highly of him," she stammered.

Eliot Carrington laughed out loud. "Two admirers in one morning isn't bad."

"Two?" Alice said, her eyes wide.

"Yes," he replied, still chuckling. "Dennis is very taken with you. He was so afraid Louise Goddard was going to let you go, he practically dragged me out of here. So if you still want the job, Miss Talbot, it's yours."

She leaned forward eagerly. "I still want it. And since Alice is my real name, will you please call me that?"

He nodded solemnly. "I will, if you'll call me Eliot, which also happens to be my real name."

Catching the twinkle in his eye, she laughed—her first laugh in over two weeks, and yet itself a heartbreaking reminder of how little she had had to laugh about.

Still, she felt she was making a little progress in her determination to put Steven out of her life. By the end of the day she was settled into her room in Eliot Carrington's apartment, ready to become an active member of the household. Though Louise Goddard was nothing more than civil to her, Alice comforted herself that in time Mrs. Goddard would unbend and become more friendly. But if she had been privy to the letter the angular housekeeper wrote that same evening to Iris Carrington, Eliot's jet-set wife, she would not have been so confident.

Suspicious as she was faithful, proud as she was devoted, if Alice had only stayed to hear Steven's reply to what Rachel said, she could have spared herself her heartbreak.

"Rachel," he had interrupted, standing up, wanting to put and end to conversation, "you've said things tonight that both of us should forget."

She followed his movement with hooded eyes. "I can't forget about you," she whispered hoarsely.

His reply was harsh. "That's too bad, because it's only

Jamie I'm interested in, not you."

With feline swiftness, she rose to her feet. "I don't believe you."

"Rachel, Jamie would never have been conceived if I hadn't been lonely and miserable and vulnerable at the time."

"I—I don't believe you," she repeated. "Steve, I love you."

He shook his head slowly from side to side. "No, Rachel. You love yourself and what you can get from other people. That's why you came here tonight. Jamie was only an excuse. You came here to get something for yourself. Well, you should have stayed home. All you've done is waste my time."

With that he showed her out of the apartment and out of the building, promising himself as he drove home that he would tell Alice at once of Rachel's visit. Only he reached home to find Alice gone.

He hurried to her parents' house as soon as he heard they'd received Alice's first letter, still unaware that Alice had overheard part of his conversation with Rachel. He could offer no explanation as to the "something so terrible" might be.

"Steve," his mother-in-law said, as they sat together in the Matthews living room, "is there something wrong between you and Alice that you haven't told us about?"

"No. Nothing"

"You're sure?" his father-in-law probed.

Steve turned to him. "Jim, I thought everything was wonderful between us. It just doesn't make sense."

"Think back over what's happened recently, Steve. You might remember something," she prodded.

Steve sighed. "I haven't thought of anything else since

17

she left. I can't come up with anything."

"Then," his father-in-law said, "surely she'll come back."

Steve passed an agitated hand across his forehead. "She's got to. She's the only thing that's ever made my life mean anything." He looked intently at Jim. "And I don't even know where she is or why she's left me."

Nor would he find out in the days and weeks that followed. By chance, he eventually learned that she had gone to his office after work to pick him up, if she had found him with Rachel, she had only to hear their exchange to know he wanted no part of the woman. He was totally stymied.

In the days and weeks that followed, he could hardly bear going home at night. There wasn't a room in that house that didn't remind him of Alice—his merry, humorous, sensitive, beautiful Alice, she of the Dresden china look, of the bright blue eyes and the taffy-colored hair. He sat on the sofa night after night staring into the cold, dark fireplace brooding about her, wondering if Rachel could have said or done something to Alice that he didn't know about.

Rachel's mother, Ada, wondered too, and put the question to her point-blank. But Rachel claimed she didn't know why Alice had left Steve, any more than anybody else did. "Though it's probably very simple," she said when her mother sat her down in her kitchen to find out what, if anything, she knew. "They probably had a fight. It's happened before."

"But," Ada protested, "they're crazy about each other."

"If they're so crazy about each other, why does Alice keep walking out on him?"

"Last time it was your fault," Ada reminded her cynically.

Rachel tossed her head, flouncing the dark hair she wore in a pageboy. With her heart-shaped face, she was extremely pretty, and knew it. "Well, this time it wasn't, no matter what you think."

Ada sighed. "All right. I'm sorry. It just seems so strange, that's all. And I hear Steve is going out of his head with worry."

"Then maybe seeing Jamie would be good for him." And she began concocting plans for him to see Jamie—and herself.

To help ease his loneliness Steve asked his sister, Janice, to come live with him. A short, slight, plain-faced girl, Janice had none of her brother's magnetic charm, or his good looks: his sensitive, square jawed face and especially the dark, brooding, eyes that made you feel when he looked at you that you that you were only person in the world.

Rachel was quick to make Janice's acquaintance, and—by criticizing Alice for walking out on Steve and generally casting her in a bad light—was just as quick to make Janice her ally.

After Alice's parents received a second letter from Alice, in which she said, "I left Steven because I found out he'd been betraying me," Janice tried to persuade her brother to give up on his wife.

"But I didn't betray her," Steven repeated as they sat together in front of the fireplace in the living room, the fire Janice had made earlier gone to embers. "I don't know what she's talking about."

Janice persisted. "Maybe her idea of betrayal and yours are two different things."

"How could that be?" Steve demanded.

Not able to meet his gaze, she answered, "I don't know.

19

But she obviously thinks one thing and you think another. That's all I meant." After a pause she turned to look at him. "I don't think she really understands you, Steve."

He rose from the sofa and poked the embers. "How can you say that? You don't even know her."

"No, I don't, but girls like that who come from nice homes and good families don't always understand people like us, even though they want to."

He turned to stare at her. "What are you trying to tell me, Janice?"

"Only that you shouldn't keep looking at what you've lost."

"Will you stop telling me I've lost Alice?" he snapped, setting down the poker. "All of her things—well, most of her things—are still here."

Janice stifled a derisive laugh. "And you think that means she'll come back? You know, Steve, for someone who's come so far in the world, you can be very naïve."

As weeks turned into months and there was still no word for him from Alice, he began to think that perhaps Janice was right—maybe he *was* being naïve. He also began to feel that Alice—who put such high marks on fairness—was being unfair to him. The least she could do was talk to him, tell him what the problem was, let him try to solve it. Was her refusal to do that a sample of her fairness to him?

Still he hoped he would hear from her, that she would come back to him—until the night her father came to collect the rest of her belongings, saying Alice had written, asking them to store her things at their house.

That was when hope died, when he finally admitted to himself that Alice was never coming back to him.

Sometime earlier, Rachel's father, Gerald Davis, had moved to Bay City to help her husband, Ted Clark, run The Hearthside Inn. At first sympathetic to Ted, Gerald came to regard him as a loser and joined Rachel's campaign to win Steve away from Alice. Sitting at the bar with her one afternoon, he told her this was no time to hang back in her campaign, "Not when it's all set up for you."

Rachel frowned at him. "What do you mean, 'it's all set up' for me?"

Realizing he had almost given himself away as the person who had left the message at the hospital for Alice, he back pedaled. "I mean, no matter why Alice has left Steve, it's up to you to make the most of it."

Rachel looked at him askance. "You know more about this than you're telling me, don't you?"

Playing the innocent, he countered, "How could I? I don't even know Alice Frame that well."

"Maybe not," she agreed, "but I get the feeling you know something I don't."

Her father spread his hands. "All I know is, you have the chance of your lifetime right now. With Alice gone, you can wrap Steve Frame around your little finger. And remember, I'm here to help you in whatever way I can."

His help was forthcoming a few nights after Jim Matthews packed up the rest of Alice's belongings and took them away, for he called Rachel to tell her Steve was there at The Hearthside Inn sitting alone in a booth and drinking. Dressing in a sexy, skintight outfit, depositing Jamie for the night at her mother's house, Rachel headed for the restaurant.

Steve looked up from his scotch and soda. "Well, hello, Rachel." His tone was neither friendly nor unfriendly.

Still unsure of herself where Steve was concerned, and trying to gauge his mood, Rachel gave him a little half smile. "Hello, Steve. Dad told me you were here."

Steve took a long pull on his drink. "I suppose you've heard what happened."

Rachael slipped into the booth opposite him. "If you mean about the Matthewses taking Alice's belongings away, yes. I'm sorry."

"Are you?" He finished his drink and set the glass down heavily. "Why should you be?"

"I don't like to see you unhappy, Steve. I care about you. I always have."

"So you keep saying." He looked around for a waiter.

Rachel put her hand on his arm. "Steve, you don't really want another drink, do you? Drinking isn't going to solve anything."

His dark eyes flashed. "Nothing's going to solve anything. Here all this time I've been waiting for Alice to come home and forgive me. Only I've never been able to figure out what she's supposed to forgive me for." He seemed exhausted by his sudden outburst. "Betraying her. I never betrayed her. I loved her. Maybe that's what needs to be forgiven. Where's the waiter?

"Steve, let me take you home."

"No!" he insisted petulantly. "I don't want to go home. I can't stand the thought of going home. I've spent too many nights alone in that great big empty house."

"Janice is there."

"I know Janice is there. Janice is no help. Not for what I need." Again he turned that brooding, intent look on Rachel. "I suppose you knew all along Alice wasn't coming back to me," Steve grumbled.

"I didn't know anything one way or the other. I still

don't." Rachel was all wide-eyed innocence.

"What do you mean, you still don't? I just told you, didn't I? Alice is never coming back. It's all over." He shook his head helplessly. "I didn't want to believe it. I've spent the last four months not wanting to believe it, but now I have to . . . Alice isn't coming back to forgive me for what I didn't do. How do you like that?" He snorted bitterly.

Rachel took a breath—and a gamble. "I've never thought Alice was right for you, Steve."

Pushing the empty glass in small wet circles on the table in front of him, he nodded. "You're probably right. No. Not probably. You *are* right. I never should have married Alice." In a swift, heart-rending movement, he buried his face in his hands.

Rachel sat silent for a few moments, then spoke softly. "Steve, let me take you home."

He mopped at his face with his handkerchief. "I'm not going home. I'm going back to the office." His voice was hard and brusque again.

"Then let me take you there."

He got up and stood looking down at her. "All right. Come along if you want."

Her heart pounding with excitement, she followed him from the restaurant. They drove to the building housing the multimillion-dollar Steven Frame Enterprise and took the private elevator up to his old bachelor apartment, where she had once before seduced him. For years she had desperately wanted to repeat that event. Perhaps tonight . . .

He fixed drinks for them, as she curled up on his leather and chrome sofa. Clicking his glass against hers, he smiled wanly. "Well, cheers—I guess."

She returned his smile. "Things will look better to you one day."

"Maybe," he said, sitting down beside her. "At least they can't get any worse." It was all she could do not to reach out to him.

"In time, Steve, you'll forget Alice."

He shook his head. "No. But maybe in time I won't give a damn anymore. Maybe I don't give a damn right now." He looked at her as he said that—more intently now—and she thought he surely must hear her heart thumping under her ribs. "One thing I know for sure," he added. "I'm not going to make the same mistake again."

"You start talking about mistakes—" she took a long, slow drink "—and you're going to wind up in my territory. I'm the champion mistake-maker."

He eyed her warily. "Like now, you mean?"

"No. Not now. I was thinking of other things . . . in the past."

"Let's forget the past," he said abruptly, "both of us. Near and far."

She still wasn't certain of him. "Are you sure you want to, Steve?"

"Yes, I'm sure." He set his drink down. Then slowly, deliberately, he took her glass from her hands and set it down next to his. When he stood up, her hand was in his and he was pulling her to her feet. "Will you help me forget, Rachel?"

It was the moment she'd been waiting for! She threw her arms around his neck. "Oh, yes, Steve. Yes." She reached to turn his face to hers, but it wasn't necessary. He was already kissing her so hard, pulling her against him so she could hardly breathe. "Oh, darling," was all she could manage. "Oh, darling."

Without another word he picked her up in his arms and carried her into the bedroom. It was their moment of passion and splendor, the moment that Rachel had hoped and planned for . . .

The sun was streaming through the half open blinds when she woke up. His half of the bed was empty and, remembering his morning after regrets the last time, she panicked. But before she could do or say anything, he came into the bedroom wearing a brown velour robe, offering her the glass of orange juice that he held in his hand.

Taking it, she said, "I thought you were already sorry you'd had me stay."

He sat down beside her. "No, Rachel. I'm not sorry. I'm glad."

She looked at him uncertainly. "Do you really mean that?" To her, he was almost unfathomable.

"Yes, I do."

She set the glass of orange juice down and held out her arms to him. When he embraced her, she sighed, "Oh, if you only knew how long I've waited to hear you say that. Oh, Steve, Steve. Love me. Please."

And he obliged her.

That night they met again in his apartment. Rachel had bought a new dress, a slinky black, strapless cocktail gown. She spun around for him. "Do you like it?"

"I like it—and you," he said.

She clung to him. "Oh, Steve, I was so scared. I thought maybe you'd changed your mind since this morning."

He pulled away from her and moved to the bar. "Well, I haven't. I've been thinking about you all day." He brought the two tonics over to the couch and sat down. "Rachel," he said, staring into his drink, "I'm ready to forget Alice."

She didn't think he sounded convinced. "Do you really mean that?"

"Yes." He still wasn't looking at her. "I can't spend my life sitting in an empty house waiting for a wife to come back to me who thinks so little of me she won't even get in touch with me to say where she is or—even more important—why she went away. Why she walked out on me. I'm grateful to you, Rachel, for helping me realize it's time I came to my senses."

In three quick little steps, she was beside him. "Then I'm glad, Steve. I've always thought if we could just have a chance, you and I . . . well . . ."

"What about Ted?"

Some weeks earlier Ted Clark had informed Rachel that he was going to leave The Hearthside Inn and move to Chicago to work in a restaurant there. He would go ahead and find a place for the three of them to live, then send for them. Rachel let him think she agreed to his plan, but she has no intention of joining him, and she said as much to Steve now, adding, "I told you before I wouldn't let Ted take Jamie away from you. Now that everything is changed, do you think I'd let him take *me* away from you?" She shook her head. "As long as you want me, Steve, you can have me."

Steve put an arm around her. "I do want you, Rachel. I want you to be with me—every night and every morning. Can you promise me that?"

"Yes."

"And I'll take care of you and Jamie. I'll take good care of you."

Rachel wanted him to be more specific. She wanted to hear the word *marry*, but he didn't mention it, and she wasn't ready to push. For all his talk about forgetting

Alice, for all her long belief that he loved her more than he had ever loved Alice, she wasn't sure he might not change his mind—as he had changed it once before.

She could wait until she was more sure of him.

Chapter Two
A Deception Revealed

Alice had hardly settled into her new job as Dennis Carrington's governess when his mother paid a surprise visit.

"Darling," she said, sweeping Dennis into her arms, "how is my winsome boy?"

"Oh, Mom," he said, clutching her and beaming with joy, "how long will you be here?"

She held him away from her to look at him. "Long enough for you to tell me how everything is with you. And how *is* everything?"

"Super," he said. "I have a new governess."

"Yes, so I've heard. Do I get to meet her?"

"Sure, Mom. You wait right here, and I'll get her." He left his mother in the bright, sunny living room and went charging to Alice's room to pound on her door. "Alice! My mom's here. Come meet her!"

Seated at the desk in her bedroom, Alice was writing a letter to her friend Lenore Curtin. "Yes, Dennis. Just a sec," she called out. Putting her pen down, she put the unfinished letter into the drawer and locked it before going to the door of her room. Dennis was standing there, his thin face flushed with excitement. "Come meet my my mom," he said. "Oh, I'm so excited!"

Alice chuckled. "Yes, I can see that. I didn't know your mother was coming today."

"Neither did I! But she hardly ever lets us know ahead of time." Grinning broadly, he grabbed Alice's wrist and tugged at her, "Come on. She wants to meet you."

Alice went with him to the living room. By this time Iris Carrington's features were well know to Alice. She had seen many pictures of her, from snapshots to studio portraits—and even, in various magazines, an endorsement of a brand of expensive perfume. Alice held out her hand. "How nice to meet you, Mrs. Carrington."

Iris replied cordially, but her private reaction to Dennis's new governess was anything but. "I've heard about you from Mrs. Goddard," she said, adding with a touch of malice, "I understand you're something of a mystery woman."

Before Alice could say anything Dennis said, "She's hiding out from the cops, Mom. She owes back income taxes."

Alice turned to him. "I thought I was an ax murderer."

Dennis shrugged. "That was yesterday."

Alice mimicked him, trying to pass over the inquiry with a light heartedness she didn't feel. "Well, at least that shows how versatile I am."

Dennis shook his head slyly. "No. It shows how versatile *I* am."

And they both dissolved in genuine laughter.

Iris laughed with them—politely. Then she frowned and said to Alice, "You don't let him get overexcited, do you?"

"No. But I try not to let him get too underexcited either,

29

Mrs. Carrington. One's as bad for his health as the other," she said, tousling the boy's hair.

"I suppose so," Iris sniffed. Any implication that she wasn't the primary expert where her son's well-being was concerned rubbed her the wrong way. Turning from Alice to Dennis she said, "Where's your father?"

The boy scratched his knee absently. "Out on a story somewhere, I guess."

"Here in New York?"

"I don't know, Mom." He appealed to Alice. "Do you know where Dad is, Alice?"

"Yes. He's in Washington, D.C., but he should be back tonight." She turned to the phone table in the corner of the room. "I have a telephone number for him in Washington if you want to call him."

Iris shook her perfectly coiffed blond head. "No. That won't be necessary. I can wait to talk to him when he gets back."

Dennis seized one of her hands. "Then you'll stay at least that long, Mom?"

She smiled down at him. "Of course, darling. Now run along, won't you? I want to talk to Miss Talbot alone."

Disappointment settled on his thin young face like a cloud across the sun, but he turned and went out of the room. Alone now with Iris, Alice was left wondering what she wanted that couldn't be broached in front of the boy.

"I understand," Iris said imperiously, "that my husband knows why you are using an assumed name."

"Yes," Alice acknowledged. "He does."

"And may I know as well?"

Iris posed the question in a way that precluded a negative answer, but nonetheless a negative answer was what Alice gave her. "I'm sorry," she added. "I don't mean to be rude, but I only told your husband what I did in order to secure this job. Even he doesn't know the full story."

Rebuffed, Iris stiffened imperceptibly. "You make it sound unsavory."

Alice responded quietly, "It isn't unsavory, only private. And now, if you'll excuse me—unless you want to talk about Dennis."

"No, that's quite all right."

But as far as Iris Carrington was concerned, it was far from being all right. This latest governess was much too attractive to be left alone with Eliot. Something would have to be done; and the sooner, the better. She summoned Louise Goddard.

"Have you found out anything about her?" she asked when she and Louise were seated together on the long yellow sofa.

Mrs. Goddard shook her mousy brown head. "No, nothing. The other day, when she took Dennis to Central Park, I looked through her room. But she keeps her desk drawer locked, and whatever papers she has must be in there. There wasn't anything anywhere else."

Iris was thinking furiously—Alice was a threat to her realm and she felt a desperate need to get the upper hand. "Doesn't she get any mail?"

"No."

"Phone calls?"

"No."

Iris gave an exasperated sigh. "She can't have cut herself off completely from her friends and family. She must have some contact with them."

"If she makes any phone calls," Louise said, "she makes them from outside. From pay phones."

Iris thumped the sofa cushion pensively. "And you don't have another key to her desk?"

"No."

"Well," Iris said, standing up, "whatever it takes, Louise, I want to know who she really is and where she comes from. And—most important—what she's trying to hide."

"I'll do my best, Mrs. Carrington, but it may take a while."

Iris smiled down at her. "I have every confidence in you. And, Louise, are you expecting Eliot back in time for dinner tonight?"

"Yes."

"Good. Then set a place for me. It can't hurt to remind him of where his livelihood comes from—the salary that enables him to hire pretty young governesses."

If Eliot was distressed to hear on his return that his wife was in town and would be joining them for dinner, he gave no sign of it. He seemed to Alice to be indifferent to his wife—courteously indifferent. And that seemed to infuriate Iris, though no doubt for Dennis's sake she kept her feelings under tight control.

Even so, Dennis must sense the tension in the air, Alice thought. Who could not? And that night, for the first time since Alice had joined the household, he had an attack of breathlessness severe enough to require extra medication.

As for Louise's assignment of finding out who Alice was, her first break occurred at Christmas, when Alice called her parents. Listening in on an extension in her room, Louise heard Mary Matthews say, "Everybody in Bay City asks about you, darling. They all want to know when you're coming home." As soon as Alice hung up,

Louise dialed the long-distance operator and learned which Bay City Alice had made her collect call to.

A few days later she picked up a roll of film Eliot had left to be developed, but giving it to him, she ordered an extra snap shot, one he'd made of Alice in front of the Christmas tree. As soon as she could arrange it, Louise Goddard, on the pretext of visiting a sick sister in St. Louis, went to Bay City to find out who Alice really was.

It was almost stupefyingly easy. She only to to show Alice's picture a few places before somebody said, "Why, that Alice Matthews—I mean Alice Frame, now that she's married."

Louise had noticed several signs at construction sites with the name Frame on them, and she had only to ask a couple more questions to learn that Alice's husband was Steven Frame, the multimillionaire businessman.

Arranging a meeting with Steven Frame was a little more difficult. On her first visit to the office, Louise learned to her chagrin that he was out of town, and wouldn't be back until the following day. Dutifully, Louise returned the next day, only to find he wasn't "available." "I'm sorry," his secretary apologized, "but Mr. Frame usually doesn't meet with people without an appointment. If you'd like to talk to one of his administrative assistants . . ."

Louise shook her haughty head. "Just tell him I have some information about his wife."

Impassive, the secretary picked up her telephone and passed along the message. Cradling it, she said, "He'll be with you in a few minutes. If you'll take a seat over there."

The few minutes stretched into nearly half an hour, and Louise was about to protest to the secretary, when the intercom buzzed. The secretary spoke a few quick words and then said to Louise, "You can go in now."

Louise had expected an executive type, and she wasn't disappointed. Steven Frame was tall and craggy, with a firm jaw and riveting dark eyes, but his manner was no-nonsense. *Well*, she thought, *I'm not here to waste his time.* Sitting in the large chair facing his desk, she spoke. "I told your secretary I have information about your wife, and I do." She took the photo of Alice out of her bag and handed it to him. "If that's who this young lady is."

He looked at the picture and handed it back to her. "Yes, that's who she is." Then his brow darkened. "But if you know my wife, don't you know her name?"

"I do now. I didn't before. She uses the name Talbot. Miss Alice Talbot."

He seemed to flinch at her us of "*Miss.*"

"She's living and working in New York City," Louise went on. "She works for—"

His intercom buzzed. "Excuse me," he said and picked up his phone. "Yes, Pam?" He listened, then sighed. "All right, put her on." Another slight pause, then, "Yes, Rachel, what is it?" A longer pause this time, then, "Rachel, I have someone with me in the office. I'll have to get back to you, but I would think we could do that, yes. Sit tight and I'll call you right back." He hung up the phone and sat looking at Louise. No. Not at her— through her, as though he were a million miles away. A change had come over him, exactly what she couldn't define, but she was astonished to hear him say, "I'm sorry for having taken up your time, Mrs. Goddard, but I'm not interested in whatever information you might have about my wife." He stood up, came around the desk, and walked to the door of the outer office. "And now if you'll excuse me . . ."

Taken aback, she had no choice but to get up and leave. This man Alice had taken such pains to hide herself from seemed to want to have nothing to do with her! Returning to the hotel where she was staying, Louise called the airport and made a reservation on the next flight back to New York. There was no point in staying on in Bay City, She had learned all she needed to know.

Back in New York, she called Iris Carrington, then met with her in Iris's hotel suite, where she recounted her meeting with Steven Frame.

Iris stared at her in disbelief. "He didn't even want to know who she works for?"

Louise shook her head emphatically."Not after he took that phone call, no. It may have been something this Rachel person said to him, though she hardly spoke two minutes. All I know is, something changed him, and he said he wasn't interested. He showed me out, and that was that."

What had happened, of course, was that Rachel's phone call had reminded Steve—if reminder he needed—of his vow to forget Alice, to put her out of his life, to make a new life for himself with Rachel and their son, Jamie.

Iris didn't know that, at least not yet—nor would she have cared if she had known. Her only concern was Alice's availability and her physical presence in Eliot's apartment. Iris wasn't at all certain that she wanted to be reunited with her husband, but she wasn't about to hand him over to another woman, and particularly not to little Alice Matthews Frame, R.N.

"I think you're worrying for nothing, Iris," Louise said. "I don't like the girl, and I never have, but I don't think she's interested in Eliot."

"She could get interested," Iris mused. "And he's

certainly taken with her. That I can tell."

"Yes," Louise conceded reluctantly. "I'd have to agree with you there. He's most definitely taken with her."

Iris got up and went to the window overlooking Central Park South. "I wish I could think of what to do."

"I'm sure," Louise said, "some opportunity will present itself."

And it did, in a very short time.

Very soon after the new liaison was established between Rachel and Steve Frame, Rachel's mother, Ada, went to see Steve in his office. She was indignant, and she made no bones about it. Refusing to sit down, she stood in front of his desk, clenching its edge. "You're taking advantage of Rachel, Steve, and you know it," her voice hammered at him angrily. "You're lonesome for Alice and feeling sorry for yourself, and you know as well as I do that Rachel would lie down and let you walk all over her if you just say the word. Isn't it bad enough that your own marriage seems to be breaking up? Do you have to break hers up as well?"

Steve eyed her coolly. "Rachel doesn't want to stay with Ted."

Ada jumped on her reply. "Of course she doesn't, with you bedazzling her out of her wits! And what kind of security can you offer her? Has Alice divorced you?"

He sighed. "I haven't heard a word from Alice, Ada. You know that."

"Al right, then. She's still your wife, and Rachel is still Ted's wife."

"That can change."

"Yes," Ada agreed, "it can. But will it?"

"Ada, Alice is never coming back, and apparently Ted

isn't coming back either," Steve insisted.

"Maybe not, but at least Ted wants Rachel with him."

Now Steve stood up, walking behind his chair to lean on it, facing her. "Well, she doesn't want to go. She wants to stay here with me, and I want her to stay here with me."

Ada grimaced. "You want her to stay here with you in what capacity? Are you talking about sneaking in and out of bedrooms together, or are you talking about marrying her?"

"I'm talking about making a home for her and Jamie."

She didn't take her eyes off his face. "A home with you in it?" she persisted.

"Yes, a home with me in it."

For a few moments she only looked at him. Then she said, marveling, 'You'd do all that for Jamie."

Steve frowned. "I don't know what you mean."

"I'm saying it plain enough," she said impatiently. "It isn't Rachel you want, Steve—except to satisfy your . . . needs. It's Jamie. If you could have Alice and Jamie both, you wouldn't give Rachel a second look."

"That's not true," Steve said lamely.

For her part, Ada couldn't convince Rachel that Steve wouldn't marry her. "He will, Mom," Rachel said. "He's said over and over he wants to make a home for the three of us, and how can he do that without marrying me?"

But Rachel wasn't as confident as the front she put on to her mother. As Ada had pointed out, she and Steve had talked more than once about her getting a divorce from Ted, but so far he hadn't said anything about divorcing Alice. Still, deciding to get things moving, she wrote Ted, asking for a divorce. And whenever she could, she talked to Steve about the life they were going to have together, dissatisfied by the vagueness and generalities of his answers, but fearful of pushing him too hard too soon.

Six months after leaving Steven, Alice still had told nobody where she was living or what she was doing. Then in the middle of March she saw an article in *The New York Times* about a medical convention being held at the Waldorf, and her brother was listed as one of the physicians attending it. On impulse—and feeling terribly homesick—she called him and made a dinner date for the following night.

She was sorry almost immediately after hanging up the phone, convinced that merely the sight of Russ she would dissolve into tears and give in to his entreaties to return to Bay City. Having done that, she wouldn't have the strength to withstand her husband's entreaties to come back to him, to his promises that if he had betrayed her before, he wouldn't again—promises all made and broken before.

Still, she met Russ in the Oak Room at the Plaza, impressed as always by its dark wood-paneled walls, the graciousness of the waiters, most of them older men. She did nearly dissolve into tears when, spying her from one of the tables, Russ got up to greet her, looking taller and leaner than ever. He smiled his old sweet smile at her, and when he took her in his arms and hugged her, she thought her heart might break. But in the flurry of their greetings and ordering their drinks she managed not to break down, and after she'd had a few sips of white wine, she felt a bit more relaxed and under control.

He asked almost immediately about Steven.

"I don't want to talk about him, Russ," she said. I'm going to forget him."

Her brother raised his eyebrows skeptically. "By running

away from him? By ignoring the truth?'"

She took another sip of wine. "By however I have to do it."

He waited before replying, gathering his thoughts. The murmurs of low conversation and the chink of sliver and glass drifted around them. "Alice, you've always run away from things."

"I know that."

"It's no solution."

She remained stubbornly silent.

Reaching across the table, Russ squeezed her hand. "Alice, come home. Mom and Dad miss you. We all miss you."

She pulled her hand away abruptly and blinked back the hot tears filling her eyes. "Russ, please. Don't ask me to come home. I miss all of you too. You must know that. But I have to make a new life for myself. I *am* making a new life for myself. I have a very nice job working for a very nice man . . ."

Russ frowned. "Doing what?"

Alice fidgeted with her fork. "I'm not ready to give out any information yet. Russ, please. Trust me. Be patient."

Melting at her entreaty, he smiled gently again. "O.K., Alice. We'll all be patient. Take your time."

She had to swallow a few times before she could say what came next, but she managed it. "Tell Mom and Dad I'm fine, and I'm—I'm happy."

"And Steve?"

"I told you before. I don't want to talk about him."

Russ acquiesced. "All right. But, Alice, there is one thing I think you ought to know. He's seeing Rachel."

She had been prepared for that, determined not to let it upset her. "I'm not surprised," she said. "He was seeing

Rachel before I left him."

A flash of orange at her elbow made Alice turn. Iris Carrington had appeared out of nowhere and was standing at their table. "Hello, Alice," she said.

"Hello," Alice said, deliberately not using her name.

Iris waved a hand toward the mahogany bar that ran almost the length of the room. "I'm with that group of people over there—and I saw you and just wanted to say hello."

"Well," Alice said awkwardly, "hello again." She felt like an idiot, but Iris Carrington must have felt like one too because after a deliberate glance at Russ, she made some other superficial remark and went back to her friends.

"Who is she?" Russ asked.

"Someone who knows the man I work for."

Russ grinned. "What have you got against her?"

"Is it that obvious?"

"It is to me."

Alice turned to look at Iris, then to her brother. "She's a schemer, and you know how I feel about schemers."

He raised his wineglass. "I'll drink to that."

When Russ returned to Bay City from the cardiology convention in New York, he stopped by Steve's office to tell him about his dinner with Alice. "She pretends she's happy, Steve, but I dont' think she is."

Sitting behind his massive desk, Steve said nothing for a few moments, nor could Russ tell what he was thinking. Finally he said, "Russ, I've never heard one word from her—why she left me, where she went, what she's doing, how she feels. I waited and waited to hear something from her. Anything." He seemed terribly pained but continued. "Finally I stopped waiting. It's as simple as that. Whatever

Alice may feel or not feel, my life has changed now."

Russ hesitated. "You mean you're not interested?"

Still he sat silent. Finally he said. "Yes, that's right."

"I understand," Russ said, "that you're seeing Rachel again."

The remark aroused Steve's listless gaze to smoldering intensity, but exactly what emotion had been tapped, Russ couldn't tell. He sounded angry, though, when he countered, "Well? What of it?"

Russ felt he was treading on dangerous ground, but as long as he had opened the subject, he would carry through. "Is Rachel the reason Alice left you?"

Steve snorted with disgust. "I wasn't 'seeing' Rachel—as you put it—before Alice left me. So how could she be the reason?"

"Alice said you were."

"Well, she's wrong. I wasn't."

"I'm sorry," Russ said, genuinely saddened. "I suppose it's none of my business."

He expected Steve to deny, but Steve said coldly, harshly, "That's right. It isn't."

With that, Russ got up to leave, but heading for the door he turned back. "All right, Steve. But someday you'll find out what Rachel is really like. And then God help you."

Still seated at his desk, Steve said, "I already know what Rachel is really like. I found that out a long time ago."

For a long moment Russ stared at his brother-in-law, then turned and left the room.

For the last several weeks Steve had been trying to sell The Hearthside Inn. He had bought it as an investment in Ted Clark, hoping thereby to keep Rachel's marriage to him stable—and to keep her from meddling in his own. Since the marriage was as good as finished now, and since Ted had gone to live and work in Chicago, Steve saw no point in hanging on to the place, but he was having trouble finding a buyer for it. Rachel was insisting that her father staying on as its manager had to be part of the deal. One morning at the end of March she stopped by the restaurant to tell her father she thought Steve had finally found a buyer, only to be told by her father that he was leaving Bay City and going to San Francisco.

Rachel stared at him, horrified. "San Francisco? But that's clear across the country!"

In that moment Rachel strongly resembled the dark-haired, dark-eyed man who was her father. Unaffected by her reaction, though, he merely shrugged and said, "I have to go where I can get a job, and I've got one in San Francisco."

Rachel had spent most of her life dreaming about her father, this man who had abandoned Ada and her when she was only a baby. She had finally unearthed him in Somerset, a town not far from Bay City, and had thereafter lured him to Bay City, where she had managed to have a more or less satisfactory relationship with him. He hadn't exactly turned out be the father of her dreams, but he was better than no father at all. Now she was about to lose him again, something she didn't like one bit.

"And it doesn't bother you to walk out of here and leave me?" she pouted.

He cleared his throat. "I didn't say that."

"You don't have to say it." She tossed her dark head, adding, "Mom was right about you. The only person you care anything about is you. You certainly don't care anything about *me*."

This daughter of his had stumped him from the first time she walked into his restaurant in Somerset and told him who she was. "Rachel, honey, that's not true."

"Isn't it? Aren't you doing the same thing to me now you did to me when I was a baby? Things aren't going a hundred percent for you, so you pack up and leave."

He was beginning to sweat a little; he didn't like scenes. "Rachel, you're a grown woman now, married and with a child of your own. It isn't the same at all."

She wasn't appeased. "Just because I'm grown doesn't mean I don't care anything about you."

With this, he thought he saw an opening. "And just because I'm leaving doesn't mean I don't care anything about you. I do care. I want you to come and see me. I expect to come back here to see you." He walked over to the coffee machine and poured out two cups of coffee. "Come on. Sit down with me and have a cup of coffee."

He led the way to a table. She followed him but sat as far from him as she could, sulkily stirring cream and sugar into her coffee.

"How are things going with you and Steve?" he ventured.

She shrugged. "O.K."

"Only O.K.? Not sensational? Come on, Rachel, don't stay mad at your old man," he cajoled.

Staring down into her coffee cup, she said, "I thought once you came here you were going to stay."

He sipped his coffee. "I thought so too, but things don't always work out the way they're supposed to. Look, honey, how many times have you talked to me about living your life on your own terms? Well, I have a life too, you know."

Setting the spoon in the saucer, she answered slowly, "I

know that. But San Francisco—"

"And anyhow, you don't need me anymore, now that I've fixed things up for you and Steve."

Rachel's hand stopped in midair and she looked up, apprehensive. "What do you mean, you fixed things up for me and Steve?"

"Helped fix things up," he amended lamely.

She searched his face for a clue to his uneasiness. "I still don't know what you mean."

That was when he finally told her how he had called the hospital and left the message for Alice to come by Steve's office, the day she left him.

Rachel was incredulous. "But she didn't come!"

"Oh," her father said, "I think she did. She must have. What else would explain her leaving that way? And saying what she did in that letter to her folks about Steve betraying her? She must have come to the office and heard you and Steve talking. Or maybe it was enough just seeing the two of you together."

"Oh, my God," Rachel said.

Her father frowned. "What's the matter?"

She looked at him, wild-eyed. "What's the matter? What happens to me if Steve finds this out?"

He was perplexed. "Why should Steve find out? The only two people who know anything about it are you and me, and we're not going to tell him."

That didn't put Rachel's fears to rest. "What about the nurse at the hospital? She knows. And Alice—she knows."

"They don't know it was me."

"They don't have to," Rachel said. "They'll think it was me putting somebody up to it, and if Steve ever finds *that* out, I'm finished. Oh, why in the world did you ever do a thing like that?" she whimpered.

Her father stared, unable to believe his ears. "To give you a chance at Steve Frame. And it worked, didn't it? Aren't you spending almost every night with him? Isn't it just a matter of time until he's divorced Alice and married you?"

Rachel shook her head. "Maybe, but it sure won't be if Steve finds out what you've done."

"Rachel, honey, relax. If Steve didn't find it out right after Alice left him, when he was practically tearing his town apart trying to figure out why she'd walked out on him, why do you think he's going to find it out now? Hell, he doesn't even care about her anymore."

"I don't know . . ." she said uncertainly.

"Don't give me that. You're in a better position than anybody else to know who he cares about these days. And it's you, not Alice. Isn't that so?"

"Yes," Rachel admitted. "But for how long?"

Gerald finished his coffee. "For as long as you want him to care about you, that's how long."

Rachel hugged herself, as if she were cold. "I hope so."

Her father smiled. "I know so."

But despite her father's assurances, Steve would one day learn the truth—and, ironically, Gerald Davis would be the one to tell him.

Chapter Three
The End of a Dream

When Iris Carrington and Louise Goddard agreed that Eliot was very taken with Alice, they were right. But he was also aware that she was grieving and bottling up her grief, and that she was still very much bound to the husband she had run away from. For the time being, he offered her friendship and compassion, and hoped the day would come when he could offer her a relationship more intensely personal—and she could accept that offer. In newspaper circles Eliot was tough and hard-driving. But at home, in his relationships with his son and with Alice, he was kind and considerate, thoughtful as well as sensitive.

One afternoon shortly after the cardiology convention in New York, Eliot asked Alice to come to his study. Leaving Dennis with his homework, she reported to her employer, who told her he had decided to take a few days vacation and that Dennis would go with him. Alice was enthusiastic. "Oh, Eliot, how nice. He'll be so thrilled. You're gone so much of the time, and he does get lonely."

He nodded. "Yes, I know that. Now what about it from

a medical standpoint? What do you think his doctor will say?"

Alice smiled. "I think his doctor will be as pleased as I am—as long as he takes his medication and doesn't over-exert himself. I'll write out all the instructions for you."

That last remark of Alice's gave Eliot a better idea—she must come on the vacation with them. At first she hesitated, arguing that Dennis and his father needed to have time together, but when Eliot pointed out that if she were along she could see to it herself that Dennis didn't overdo, she agreed to go with them, that is, until she found out where Eliot was planning to take them—to a friend's house on the island of St. Croix.

"Oh, no," she said, horrified. "No, I couldn't possibly. No, no, I—"

He was mystified. "Alice, what is it? What's wrong?"

Agitated, she ran a hand through her taffy-colored hair. "That's where we—I—Steven and I—we spent our honeymoon there. No, I couldn't possibly." She turned and ran out of the room.

After dinner that night Alice asked Eliot if she could speak to him privately. "Yes, of course," he said. He went with her to the study and closed the door, waving her to a chair. "What is it?" he asked kindly.

She swallowed. "I want to know if I may still go to St. Croix with you and Dennis."

He smiled. "Well, of course you may. I'm delighted to hear it." But as he looked at her, his concern deepened. "Are you sure you want to?"

"Yes," she stated. "I am. The other night I had dinner with my brother. He's a doctor—a cardiologist—and he was here in New York to attend a medical meeting. His name is Russell Matthews. That was my name before I married. Matthews. My husband's name is Steven Frame."

Eliot asked quietly, "Why are you telling me all this?"

Her reply tumbled out, carried by her pent up feelings. "Because I want you to know. Because I'm going to stop hiding and I'm going to stop running. That was something Russ—my brother—told me the night I had dinner with him. He said I've always run away from things, and he's right. I've got to stop it. That's why I've decided to go to St. Croix with you and Dennis . . . if you still want me to come. I mean, knowing that—well, it won't exactly be easy for me. Maybe under the circumstances you'd rather I didn't—"

But Eliot didn't agree with that. He told her she had made a wise decision, and though he realized this was going to be hard for her, he was willing to give her any help she might require.

The one thing Alice felt she didn't need—and couldn't cope with, even with Eliot's help—was the possibility of encountering Steven on St. Croix. To make sure he wouldn't be there, she called her sister Pat, who was married to John Randolph, Steven's legal adviser. It would be easy enough for John to ask Steven what his schedule would be the following week.

Steve had said he expected to be in Bay City, news that was quickly relayed back to Alice. Suffused with pleasure and relief, she set out to shop for the tropical clothing she would need. While she was doing that, Louise Goddard was telling Iris what was in the wind. Iris was predictably dismayed.

"What are you going to do?" Louise asked bluntly.

Iris frowning, paced back and forth across her hotel living room. "I don't know. But something." Then her face let up and she snapped her fingers. "I'm going to fly to Bay City tomorrow and talk to Steven Frame myself."

"What good will that do?" the housekeeper queried. "He's already told me he isn't interested in hearing about his wife."

"I know what he told you, but I don't believe it. At any rate, it's worth a try. Call the airline and make a reservation for me," she ordered.

The next afternoon Iris was seated in Steve's outer office waiting to see him when Rachel dropped in unexpectedly, as usual. Steve's secretary had become accustomed to Rachel's unannounced visits—she'd been doing it for years now—and was discreetly polite as ever, but told Rachel she would have to wait, there was somebody ahead of her. Rachel, turning to see who the somebody was, went bug-eyed. She had never seen the snapshots or studio portraits of Iris Carrington that Alice was privy to, but she *had* seen the perfume ads in various fashion magazines, and she read all the gossip columns. She knew almost as much about Iris Carrington as Iris did herself.

Rachel, never having been one to waste an opportunity to advance herself, boldly went over to Iris and held out her hand. "You're Iris Carrington, aren't you?" she announced.

Iris looked up from the magazine she was leafing through and gave Rachel a cool smile. "Yes, I am." She ignored the outstretched hand.

Flushing with embarrassment, Rachel dropped her hand and said, "Pam says you're waiting to see my fiancé—well—" she gave Iris her little self-deprecating smile—"my almost-fiancé, Steve Frame."

There was an immediate thaw in the social climate, and Iris patted the sofa cushion beside her. "Then you must be

Rachel." Iris narrowed her eyes, scrutinizing.

"Yes, I am," Rachel said, sitting beside her. "But how did you know?"

"Oh," Iris said airily, "I hear things."

Rachel didn't doubt for a moment that she had. And if people like Iris Carrington had heard about her before she and Steve were married—or even formally engaged—think what it would be like after she was Mrs. Steve Frame! She could hardly contain herself.

She wanted desperately to know why Iris was here to see Steve, but at that moment the intercom buzzed, and after speaking into the phone Pam told Iris that Mr. Frame would see her now.

While Iris was ushered into the inner office, Rachel settled back on the leather sofa. This was one time she didn't mind having to wait, and if she didn't find out from Iris Carrington what she was there for, she would find it out from Steve.

As it happened, she found it out from Iris, and in very short order.

After Louise Goddard had established who Alice was and what she was trying to hide, Iris, without saying anything to Louise, had hired a private detective to do a more thorough investigation into the Alice-Steve-Rachel triangle. The results had convinced her that Steve was still very much in love with Alice and would do anything to have her back. Armed with that conviction, she now introduced herself to Steve, saying Alice worked for her husband, Eliot Carrington, and that Steve should go after his wife before Eliot had a chance to "influence her too much," were the words she used.

"Mrs. Carrington," Steve said, "you could have saved yourself time and energy by calling me by phone to have this conversation. I'm no longer interested in going after my wife. That's all there is to it."

His intercom buzzed. Picking up the phone he said, "Yes, Pam? My Los Angeles call? Good. Put him on. No. Wait a second." Covering the mouthpiece, he said to Iris, "I'm sorry. This is a call I have to take."

Her eyebrows arched. "Do you want me to wait outside?"

He shook his head. "I don't want you to wait at all, Mrs. Carrington. I have nothing further to say to you. Now, if you'll excuse me." He uncovered the mouthpiece. "All right, Pam. Put him on."

Iris rose and stalked out. She was furious and made no attempt to hide her feelings.

"My goodness," Rachel said, looking up startled, "that didn't take long, did it?"

"Long enough to know I wasn't welcome," Iris said archly. "I wanted to tell your almost-fiancé that his wife and my husband are flying to St. Croix together the day after tomorrow, but he wasn't interested."

This was almost too much news for Rachel to absorb at one time; she couldn't help staring. "Alice knows Eliot Carrington—I mean, your husband?"

Iris sniffed. "She works for him. She takes care of our son, Dennis."

"And they're going to St. Croix together? Did you tell Steve that?"

"Didn't I just say he wasn't interested?" She was eyeing Rachel closely. "But you can tell him for me that if Alice thinks going to St. Croix with my husband is going to do her any good, she's very much mistaken, because I have no intention of divorcing Eliot." She turned and started out of the office.

Rachel scrambled to her feet. "Mrs. Carrington, wait. I—there's something I—" Seeing that the haughty socialite had turned back to her, Rachel said hurriedly over her shoulder to Pam, "I'll be back to see Steve later," then she left the office with Iris. Once outside, she said, "Look, can we talk? I mean, you probably don't know that Steve has a house on St. Croix, and if I can get him to take me there—I mean, he wouldn't go if he knew ahead of time that Alice was going to be there. Or at least I don't think he would, but—well, is there some place we can go and talk?"

"Yes," Iris said, her curiosity piqued, "we can go back to my hotel room."

Back in New York that evening, reporting to Louise Goddard on her trip, Iris practically chortled, "It's going to be perfect. As soon as Steve Frame sees Alice with Eliot, he'll take her away from him, and that will be the end of that."

But Louise was dubious. "What if Rachel can't persuade Steve to go to St. Croix?"

Iris gestured dismissively. "She's already persuaded him. She's not the brightest creature you'll ever meet, but she is actually pretty in a common sort of way, and she's also extremely sexy. She just told him that if they went to St. Croix they could really be alone together." Then she shrugged. "And anyhow, who knows? Maybe business is slow right now, or maybe he feels in need of a vacation—or maybe he really does want to be alone with her. Whatever the reason, they're going, so all we have to do is sit back and wait for the outcome."

But she was in for a disappointment.

The night of their arrival Steve took Rachel to Louie's, a native restaurant. They were eating dinner when he happened to look up and see Alice come in with a man he didn't know. The sight of her astonished him so, he simply sat and stared in disbelief. Then he pushed back from the table. "It's Alice," he said. "I have to go speak to her."

Rachel's heart sank. "Don't, Steve," she said. "What do you expect to accomplish?"

"I don't know. I just know I have to speak to her."

Rachel grabbed his hand. "But what will you say?"

"I don't know. Let go of me, Rachel."

Withdrawing her hand, she watched anxiously as he crossed the room. In plotting this confrontation with Iris, Rachel was gambling, and she knew it. For all her conviction that Steve loved her more than he had ever loved Alice, she couldn't shake her fear that Steve still wanted Alice and would reconcile with her if he could. She had come to St. Croix with a now-or-never feeling, and the now was upon her.

Steve was speaking to Alice. Rachel couldn't hear them, though, and unable to bear it any longer she went over to join the two of them just inside the front door— Eliot Carrington having stepped over to the checkroom.

"Hello, Alice," Rachel said with a wavering smile. "Isn't this a funny coincidence?"

Alice neither answered nor looked at her. Eliot Carrington came up just at that moment so she spoke to him instead, "Shall we go to our table now?"

"Yes," he answered and led her away, neither of them looking back.

Rachel and Steve stood watching them. Finally, steeling herself, Rachel said, "You'd think she could at least have said hello . . . But then, maybe she was too embarrassed. I mean, being here with some other woman's husband."

Rachel sniggered nervously. "But then I am too, aren't I?"

Steve turned to her with a blank look. "I'm sorry. What did you say?"

"Never mind. What did you say to Alice?"

"I asked her why she left me. She didn't answer."

Rachel sniffed. "I told you you wouldn't accomplish anything. Are you coming back to the table with me to finish dinner, or are you just going to go on standing there?"

"Sorry," he said. "Let's go back to the table." Once there he signaled a waiter, then asked him, "Who's that man with the beautiful blond lady over their?"

"Eliot Carrington," the waiter said. "The newspaper columnist."

"I could have told you that," Rachel said when the waiter was gone. "You remember when Iris Carrington came to see you the other day?"

"Yes," Steve said, knitting his brow. "What about it?"

"She told me Alice is having an affair with her husband."

That got a rise out of him. "Alice having an affair?"

Rachel's chin went up in her familiar gesture of defiance. "That's what I said, yes."

On the one hand, provoking any kind of response from Steve was gratifying. On the other hand, she didn't like the fact that about all he really responded to was any mention of Alice.

Just at the edge of his field of vision, Steve could see Alice's taffy colored hair. "I don't believe it," he said. "Alice isn't that kind of a person."

The chin rose a notch. "Meaning I am?"

He didn't answer.

Rachel began to wish she hadn't talked Steve into

coming to St. Croix, but at least she didn't seem to be coming out the loser. Alice and Eliot left the restaurant before they did, she and Steve staying on and dancing after dinner. Then they walked back to his house hand-in-hand along the beach, and when they got there he made love to her, passionate love, as she willed him to erase Alice from his mind, to want to possess her alone.

But even Rachel couldn't banish thoughts of Alice, and the next day, telling Steve she was going shopping, she went instead to see her rival for Steve's attentions.

Eliot answered the door, not certain that Alice should see her, but Alice assured Eliot that she could handle her. She had been expecting Rachel, and kept her doubts to herself.

At first Rachel tried, as usual, to ingratiate herself with Alice, but when that didn't work, she came right to the point.

"I just wanted to tell you," she said, standing just inside the door, Alice having refused to ask her to sit down, "that Steve and I are in love with each other."

Alice was stony-faced. "If that's all you came to say, Rachel, you can leave. I'm not the least bit interested in you or Steven."

"Why wouldn't you talk to him last night?"

"That's none of your business, Rachel. Or maybe it is. He wanted to know why I left him. I think you know the answer to that."

Rachel gave her a deprecating look. "If you're talking about my being in the apartment with Steve that time, it was only about Jamie."

"Was it really?" Alice said sarcastically. "That was your only interest in being with Steven, Rachel? You had no designs on him at all?"

Rachel tossed her head. "I didn't come here to be insulted," she spat, her anger rising.

Alice reached behind Rachel and opened the door. "You had no business coming here at all. Now go, Rachel."

But Rachel didn't budge. "I haven't finished with what I came to see you about. If you're not interested in Steve anymore, then you don't love him. Right?"

"Brilliant, Rachel. Positively brilliant. But then you always were a mental giant, weren't you?"

Rachel's cheeks flushed. "If you don't love him, will you give him a divorce?"

That hit home. The color drained from Alice's face. "Did Steven send you here to ask me that?"

"No."

"Did he know you were coming here to ask me that?"

"Well—not exactly."

"What do you mean, Rachel, 'not exactly'?"

Though she thrust her chin out defiantly, Rachel felt a little frightened that the moment of confrontation had finally arrived. "Steve wants to make a home for me and Jamie. He's told me that over and over. He wants the three of us to be together. But how can he do that as long as he's still married to you?"

"If Steven wants a divorce from me—for whatever reason—he can ask for it himself."

"Jamie has a right to know Steve is his father," Rachel countered evasively.

Alice paused and frowned. "I don't get the connection. I've never said Jamie didn't have the right to know that. As far as I know, nobody's prevented you from telling him."

"I don't want him to know while his father is married to somebody else. I want his father to be married to me."

Alice nudged the door wider. "Then you're wasting your time, Rachel. I'm sorry about Jamie, but if you think I'm going to give Steven a divorce so you can move in, forget it. Now get out of here."

This time Rachel went.

As soon as Steve and Rachel returned to Bay City she called Iris Carrington in New York to make her excuses. Because Iris could introduce her to all kinds of people, all kinds of *important* people, she very much wanted Iris as a friend. "I did everything I could to see that Alice and Steve were thrown together," she said plaintively. "But she wouldn't talk to him, even when he talked to her. She just looked right through him."

"Damn," Iris muttered into the phone.

"I'm really sorry, Iris. But I also don't think you have anything to worry about. About Alice and Eliot, I mean. I mean, they weren't the least bit lovey-dovey. They didn't even dance together the night we were all at the same restaurant."

"I suppose that's encouraging. Well, thanks for trying, Rachel."

"Sure, Iris. Any time. And you will keep in touch with me won't you?"

"Why, yes, Rachel. Of course." But she sounded vague, as if Rachel were already somebody in her past.

Rachel also began pressing Steve to ask Alice for a divorce, using the same tack with him that she had tried with Alice. But while Alice merely felt sorry for Jamie, Steve was increasingly anxious to let the boy know he was his father, and finally, by the end of April, Steve told John Randolph to ask Alice to let him file for a divorce.

John had come to Steve's office that day about some

other legal matters. A teddy bear of a man, with brown hair and brown eyes, he had a friendly, open countenance. He was a good friend and a good lawyer. Putting the papers in his briefcase he said, "I'm sorry to hear this, Steve."

Steve perched on his massive desk. "Yeah—well—I never would have ever believed it would ever come to this, but it has. I guess Alice wasn't the right person for me."

John looked up sharply. "Why do you say that?"

He shrugged. "Apparently she expected something out of me that I couldn't give her. At least Rachel won't do that."

"Then you intend to marry Rachel?"

"I want Jamie to know I'm his father. I want him to grow up with both his parents."

"That's not much of a reason for marrying somebody," John responded slowly.

Steven's shoulders sagged. "All right. I love Rachel."

"You don't say that with much conviction."

Steve eased himself off the desk. "Rachel and I will be O.K. We understand one another—something Alice and I didn't do too well." He walked with John to the door. "Let me know what Alice's reaction is."

At the door John turned to him. "Do you think she'll resist giving you a divorce?"

"I don't have any idea, John. As long as I've known Alice, I've never known how she would react to anything. If I had, maybe we wouldn't be where we are now."

Alice's answer to Steve's request was no.

John had flown to New York to see her, taking Pat with him. But it was he who talked to Alice alone in their hotel room that evening.

"I have no intention of giving him a divorce," Alice said, vehemently. "I could have told you that on the phone and saved you a trip."

John shook his head at her impassioned reply. "I understand how you feel, Alice—"

She turned on him. "If you understood how I feel you wouldn't be here in this hotel room asking me what you're asking."

He studied her a moment. "Alice, so you want me to try to effect a reconciliation?"

She shook her head.

"Because of pride?"

"No." Her voice was small and tired. "When I saw Steven and Rachel together in St. Croix, I realized I'd lost him. If I ever had him in the first place."

"Alice," John said, "he only turned to Rachel out of desperation. He's never turned to her for any reason." He put a hand on her arm. "Let me speak to him."

Alice was adamant. "No. I don't want him back. Not now. Not after—" She shook her head. "No."

"Then divorce him, Alice."

"No."

"Let him file, then."

"No. John, I am not going to hand him over to Rachel. She doesn't love him. The only reason she wants to marry Steven is to get her hands on all that money, and I'm not going to let her do that."

Try as he would, John couldn't budge her.

Later, as he and Pat were getting ready for bed, Pat said to him, "In spite of what she said, darling, I think Alice still loves Steven."

John turned from the dresser where he was emptying his pockets. "What has she said to you?"

Pat smiled. "Oh, the opposite, of course. She doesn't love him, she could never forgive him—all that." She sighed deeply. "She was very insistent on it."

John started unbuttoning his shirt. "I know what you mean. Steve's the same. He no longer loves Alice, he doesn't understand her, she wan't the right person for him. You can almost see his blood pressure go up as he says it." He took off the shirt and tossed it onto a nearby chair. "Still, I don't think they'll ever get together again. They're both too proud and stubborn. They always have been, and neither of them is going to change."

The next morning John met once more with Alice, but to no avail, so that night he and Pat flew back to Bay City. In the end, it was Eliot Carrington who resolved the impasse.

The following night, after dinner, he asked Alice if he could speak to her in the study. When they were both seated, he behind his desk, she in the leather chair facing him, he said, "I want to tell you something from my own experience, Alice. May I?"

"Yes of course."

"You know that I work for my father-in-law."

Alice nodded. "Yes. Mrs. Goddard told me that quite some time ago."

Eliot toyed with a pencil rolling it between his fingers. "When I first went to work for him all those years ago, Mac—his name is Mackenzie Cory—Mac took quite a fancy to me, to my work and to me as a prospective husband for his daughter, Iris. I was young, I was flattered. And Iris is a very attractive woman—was even more so as a girl. What irritates me now I found exciting then. If you can understand."

Alice nodded again. "Yes. I mean, I know how feelings

can change," she said thoughtfully.

Eliot put the pencil down. "All right. The point I'm trying to get at is I got trapped into a corner . . . I let myself get trapped. Mackenzie Cory signed me to an exclusive contract. I can break it, of course, but if I do, I can't work for anybody else for five years. Mac could break the contract only Iris won't let him. And in things that concern me, Mac lets Iris have the say. Do you see what I am trying to tell you?"

"I'm not sure," Alice said frowning.

Eliots hands dropped into his lap and he leaned back in his chair. "There's nothing I'd like more than to be free of Iris, but she controls my life the same way she controls my career. She won't give me a divorce without a fight, and I can't risk what a court battle might do to Dennis. Not in his condition. Now do you see?"

"But Dennis and Jamie aren't the same," Alice said, still puzzled. "It's an entirely different situation."

"I wasn't thinking of Jamie's situation as it relates to Dennis'," Eliot said. "I was thinking of your husband's situation as it relates to mine. Do you want to keep Steven from living his life, the way Iris keeps me from living mine?"

For quite some time Alice said nothing, the only sound in the room the tick of the old mahogany mantel clock from its niche on a shelf. Finally she said, "I see."

The next morning she called John at his office and told him to go ahead with the divorce.

He couldn't believe he had heard her right. "Are you sure, Alice?"

"Yes, I'm sure."

"What made you change your mind?" he asked nonchalantly.

"Does it matter?" she asked in a sad voice.

"No. No, you're right, Alice. It doesn't matter." Just then, his intercom buzzed. "Can you hold on a minute, Alice?" he asked.

He put her on hold and punched the local button. "Yes, Sally?"

"Steven Frame is here."

"Tell him to come in." He went back to his conversation with his sister-in-law. "I'm sorry for the interruption, Alice. It was my secretary saying Steve has just come in. Do you want to talk to him?"

"No. I haven't anything to say to him."

"Do you want to talk conditions and specifications now, or do you want me to get back to you?"

The door opened, and Steve walked in. John waved him to a chair.

"There aren't any conditions or specifications," Alice was saying. "I don't want anything from him."

"You don't want to be too hasty, Alice."

At the mention of Alice's name, Steve sat up straight, his eyes riveted on the phone in John's hand.

"Of course, the house is yours."

"I don't want the house, John."

"But you own it, Alice. It's in your name."

"Then take it out of my name and put it in his. I don't want the house, John. I don't want anything to do with Steven. Anything. Do you understand me? Just send me whatever I have to sign, and I'll sign it. I want everything over and done with. Ended. Finished."

It was John's unpleasant task now to tell Steve what Alice had said. He listened without comment until John mentioned that she wanted the house signed over to him.

At that, he stood and walked over to a window looking

down on the street below. "So I gathered," was all he said. The intersection below was thick with traffic, pedestrians ambling in the warm spring sunshine, not eager to return to their offices after a morning coffee break. "Alice's dream house," he said in a somber voice. "What a stupid, romantic notion it was to begin with. Well, that's finished too now. And high time."

Chapter Four
Seeds of Discord

In the course of her investigation into who Alice was and what she was trying to hide, Iris Carrington had uncovered the fact that Alice's brother, Russell Matthews, was a cardiologist at Bay City's Memorial Hospital, and when she was given a picture of him, she realized that he was the young man she had seen with Alice in the Oak Room at the Plaza Hotel. Further investigation provided the information that he was an exceptionally bright young man with a growing reputation in the field of cardiology.

Iris, a self-centered woman, intent on satisfying her own wants and needs more than those of anybody else, nonetheless felt guilty about her son's heart defect, that somehow it was her fault he had been imperfectly formed in her womb. This guilt had taken her to doctors all over the world, but what she had heard about Russell Matthews intrigued her. She wanted him to have a look at Dennis; so she called the Bay City office from New York to set up an appointment.

Typically, she said nothing to her husband until the

appointment was made, and the details finalized.

"No, of course I don't object," Eliot said when she faced him in his den. "I'm just as eager as you are to see Dennis made whole. I just don't think you should get your hopes up, that's all."

Iris raised her hands in a gesture of helplessness. "I can hardly help that, Eliot."

Seeing this rare display of vulnerability, Eliot felt a flash of pity for her. "Well, try not to let Dennis see those hopes, then. When is the appointment for?"

"A week from Wednesday. And I only got in then because somebody else had canceled. He's a much sought-after doctor."

Eliot sighed. "Well, let's keep our fingers crossed. Do you want Alice to go with you?"

"She's supposed to be looking after Dennis, isn't she?"

"Yes. But I hate to ask her to go to Bay City, even for a few days."

Iris said petulantly, "Then don't ask her. I can manage perfectly well on my own."

"Why don't you take Louise with you?" Eliot suggested.

It was a tempting thought. With Louise along, Iris wouldn't have to concern herself with schedules or luggage or hotel reservations or meals or transportation to and from the doctor's office; but then again, with Louise along, Eliot would be left alone in the apartment with Alice, and that was a greater risk than she cared to take.

"No, thank you," she said. "I said I can manage on my own, and I will. Just tell Louise to see that Dennis is packed and ready to go next Tuesday morning. I want him rested when Dr. Matthews sees him."

When Alice told Dennis that he was going with his mother to Bay City, he seemed indifferent. "To see another doctor, I suppose," he said.

"Why do you say that?" Alice asked, intrigued.

He shrugged. "I never go anywhere with Mom for any other reason."

Alice squeezed his thin shoulder. "This isn't just another doctor, Dennis. This one is my brother, Russ."

Dennis brightened. "No kidding?"

"No kidding."

"You never told me you had a brother who's a doctor."

"There are lots of things about me I haven't told you, Dennis."

"Are you going to come with me and Mom?"

"You forget. I'm still hiding out from the cops there."

"Oh, yeah. I did forget. Well, if they ask me anything, Alice, I won't give you away."

Alice ruffled his brown hair. "Thanks a heap, Dennis. You're a real life-saver." But she wished with all her heart that she was going with them—probably, she told herself with some asperity, because she knew she wasn't going, and so her wish was safe.

Dennis' appointment with Russ consisted of an interview first with a nurse and then with the doctor, to record his medical history; and then a series of tests and X-rays, some of them in the doctor's office, more of them as an inpatient in Bay City Memorial. Then on Friday afternoon Iris took Dennis back to Russ's office for the follow-up interview.

They were seated in the waiting room when a nurse came out of Russ's office to say, "You can go in now."

"Thank you," Iris said. She stood up and turned to Dennis. "I can't imagine I'll be long, dear."

"No," the nurse said, "he wants to see both of you."

Iris's eyebrows went up. "Both of us? But that isn't the

way I—Whose idea is this, anyway?"

"That's the way Dr. Matthews wants it, Mrs. Carrington. You are both to go in."

Iris didn't like being ordered about by anybody, doctor or nurse, but she merely said, "Very well, then. Come along, Dennis."

After showing them to seats across from his desk, Russ sat down behind it, Dennis' now-bulging folder in his hands. He looked up from it to smile at both of them. "I think I have encouraging news for you."

So accustomed to hearing discouraging news from the various doctors she had consulted over the years, Iris could hardly believe what she was hearing now. She waited for him to continue.

"I'm sure you're both aware that many new developments in drug therapy have been made in the last few years. I think Dennis is ready for that kind of treatment now."

Something else Iris had been accustomed to hearing was the word *surgery*. "You mean without surgery?" she said in disbelief.

Russ nodded. "Yes. Without surgery." He held up a cautionary hand. "But Dennis will have to be hospitalized here—that is, if you want me to take his case. And he'll have to be hospitalized for some time."

Dennis spoke for the first time. "How long, doctor?"

Russ turned to him. "I can't say exactly, Dennis. But for a few months anyhow."

The boy sighed. "That long."

"Yes," Russ acknowledged, "that long. But if the treatment is successful, Dennis, and I have every reason to believe that it will be, then you won't be a semi-invalid any longer. You'll be a healthy boy."

Dennis's eyes widened. "Healthy enough to play ball?"

Russ smiled. "That's right."

A happy little gasp escaped Dennis' lips. "Oh! Super!" He turned to his mother. "When can we start, Mom?"

His mother smiled at him. "As soon as I can make arrangements with your father. And as soon as Dr. Matthews gives us the go-ahead."

Russ spread his hands. "I'm ready when you are, Mrs. Carrington."

The prospect of having a fully healthy son in a matter of a few months' time thrilled Iris. The prospect of spending those few months here in Bay City also thrilled her. If Alice had been unwilling to come back to Bay City for only a few days, she could never be talked into coming back for a few months. And once Alice was out of Eliot's household, she would be out of his life and no longer a threat to Iris. Iris couldn't think of a time when she had been more pleased.

When Eliot called Alice into his study to break the news to her about the move to Bay City, her reaction was exactly what Iris had expected it would be. "I can't possibly go with you," she said looking troubled.

Eliot nodded. "I know it's asking a lot of you, Alice. But I am asking it."

Alice stared at this man who had been so thoughtful of her, so sensitive to her difficulties.

"Not for my sake," he added hastily. "For Dennis'. The next few months are going to be the most crucial few months of his entire life. If he ever needed stability, he needs it now—in spades."

"Yes," Alice said, "I understand that, but . . ."

For a few moments they sat in silence. Then Eliot spoke. "Will you never go back to Bay City? Never see your parents again? Will you let two people you say you care nothing about dictate your life?"

"No, of course not," Alice spoke quickly. "It's just that I can't go back there now. Not this soon."

He eyed her. "Then you do still care about Steven."

"No."

"Then why is now too soon?"

She twisted her fingers together. "I don't know. I . . ." Her voice trailed off.

"Do you remember what your brother said to you about running away?"

She nodded.

"And about hiding from people you feel you can't face?"

"Yes," she said meekly.

"Isn't this more of that?"

She didn't answer right away. "Yes," she said finally, "I guess it is."

"Can you imagine how Dennis must be feeling?" Dennis was already hospitalized at Bay City Memorial. He'd been admitted right after follow-up visit to Russ's office, Iris seeing no reason to delay the start of treatment.

"Yes," Alice said, "I can imagine. He's scared and he's lonely." She stopped fidgeting and sat up straighter in her chair. "You're right, Eliot." She glanced at her watch and stood up.

Eliot frowned. "Where are you going?"

"To call Dennis to tell him I'll be there as soon as I can."

Eliot pushed his desk phone at her, and when she came to the desk to take it, put his hand on her arm. "I'll never forget you for this, Alice. Never."

She gave him a shaky smile. "And I'll probably never forget you either, Eliot—for helping me to grow up."

* * *

Humming a little tune, Iris Carrington swung into her hotel room and with a merry flourish tossed her hat on the bed. She had just come from the hospital, where she'd spent the day getting Dennis settled in. He'd been quite excited, of course, and it was only with difficulty that she'd hid her own agitated elation. And just now, she'd asked at the front desk if Eliot had arrived, learning that, yes, he'd checked in, accompanied only by his housekeeper, Mrs. Goddard. The prospect of Dennis' good health, her little triumph over Alice—she had not had such meaningful activity in a good while. She was just about to pick up the phone to see if Eliot would join her for dinner when there was a knock on the door. It was Louise Goddard.

"Louise!" she said, surprised.

"May I come in, Iris?"

"Well, of course you may." She drew Louise in, then shut the door. "Now tell me why you're here."

"I came to bring you some bad news. Alice is in town."

Iris stared at her. "Here? But Eliot checked in alone, she wasn't with him."

"She's not staying at the hotel. She's staying with her parents in their home."

"You mean," Iris said, her heart sinking, "she's going to stay on in Bay City?"

Louise nodded, a grim look on her face. "Yes. For as long as Dennis needs her—or so Eliot says."

"And what about Eliot?"

"He's here for the duration as well." Louise took off her light spring jacket and sat down in a chair beside the bed. "And I have more bad news for you."

Iris sat on the side of the bed. "Well? What is it?"

"Alice has agreed to give Steven Frame a divorce."

Iris glowered at the housekeeper. "I don't believe you," she said, stung.

Louise shrugged. "Believe me or not, it's true."

"How do you know?"

"I heard her talking on the phone to her sister. Her sister is married to John Randolph, the lawyer who's handling the divorce."

"For Alice, you mean?"

"For both of them, apparently. He's Steve Frame's lawyer."

"But I don't understand," Iris said. "The last I head from you, you said she was adamant about not giving her husband a divorce."

Louise gave Iris a sour look. "Well, guess who changed her mind."

Iris frowned. "You can't mean Eliot."

"Can't I? According to what she told her sister it was Eliot."

"Then Eliot does want to marry Alice."

"That I can't confirm or deny. She said nothing on the phone about that."

Iris could almost see her euphoria going out the window. "Why else would Eliot persuade her to get a divorce?"

"I don't know."

She got up from the bed and started pacing back and forth. "That has to be the reason."

From her chair beside the bed Louise could not but agree. "I would think so, yes."

Iris stopped abruptly. "Well, he needn't think it's going to be that easy. A second divorce is needed before he can marry her—his divorce from me. And that is one thing he's never going to get."

"Well, then," Louise said briskly, "you don't have anything to worry about, do you?"

But worry she did, and a few other things as well.

Her first move was to fly back to New York, where she packed more clothes, made a few telephone calls, and cleared her calendar of social engagements. Then she returned to Bay City, checking back into the hotel there, this time asking for a suite.

The next morning, she saw an opportunity to implement the plan she had formulated on her trip to and from New York. Going into the hotel dining room for breakfast, she saw Eliot alone at a table and went over to him.

May I join you, Eliot?" she said softly.

He looked up from his morning paper in surprise, then rose to his feet. "I thought you went back to New York."

"I did, but I came back last night." She sat down in the chair Eliot had pulled out for her. "Do you mind if I have breakfast with you?"

"No, of course not." He looked around, signaling for a waiter.

After she'd given her order, Iris said, "These next few months will be so important for Dennis—Eliot, I know we don't always get along, even in the best circumstances. But we agree when it comes to Dennis' well-being, don't we?" She looked up at him for confirmation, and he nodded.

"Good," she went on. "I've been thinking that for Dennis' sake, we should both be here during his hospitalization."

Eliot folded his paper carefully. "I think there's merit in what you say, Iris. Yes. As long as we don't quarrel or act as if we're about to."

Shrugging, she smiled over at him. "If you'll do your

best, Eliot, I'll do mine. Who knows? We may not even have to try very hard." Privately he doubted that, but he said nothing

There was no doubt at all that their being there together in Bay City mattered to Dennis. The first time they went to the hospital to see him together, he beamed at them, and when they told him they were both going to stay here for as long as it took for him to be cured, he could hardly contain himself.

Clasping his mother's hand in both his, he said, "Do you mean it Mom? Honest?"

"Yes," she said squeezing his hands. "Honest."

"That's super." He turned to Eliot. "And you too, Dad?"

Eliot nodded. "Yes, son. Well," he amended, "I'll have to take some trips here and there—the way I normally do. But Bay City will be my headquarters."

"That's really super," Dennis said.

Russ came into the room while they were there, and when he left, they walked with him into the corridor to ask how Dennis was doing.

"It's much too soon to have anything to report, really" Russ said. "But I'm glad to see that you're both going to be here. That will help him have a positive attitude toward his treatment, and a positive attitude is critical in this kind of long, drawn-out business."

Another asset, both from Russ's point of view and Dennis' was Alice. From being the boy's governess she had become literally his private nurse, working a full eight-hour shift in the hospital in and out of his bedroom, giving him the medication Russ ordered, supervising his physical therapy, hiring a tutor to keep him up on his schoolwork, and even helping him with his homework when she could find the time.

Talking to her one morning in the corridor outside Dennis' room, Russ said, "I can't tell you how glad I am to have you here, Alice. It will make a world of difference in Dennis' progress."

"I hope so," she said.

He patted her shoulder. "I know so. And I hope at not too great a cost to you."

"I don't want to talk about that, Russ."

"O.K. I just wanted you to know that if the time comes when you do want to talk about it, I'm here and ready to listen. And to do what I can to help."

She smiled gratefully at him. "Thanks," she said. "A girl couldn't be luckier to have a brother like you."

Alice had expected her to return to Bay City to be painful, but what she hadn't anticipated was how lonely she would be. Her parents were delighted to have her back with them, and she spent many evenings in their company, but Jim and Mary Matthews had a life of their own that often didn't include Alice—their weekly bridge club, their art lectures at the museum, an occasional function at the country club, business dinners. The evenings that Alice had spent with Eliot Carrington in New York were no longer possible here. It was not so much that she missed those things in and of themselves, but she'd quickly noticed that when she was alone, thoughts of Steven and Rachel occupied her mind. Many nights movies or television or books were her only distraction. But she busied herself as best she could and tried not to think about where Steven was and what he was doing, and was Rachel doing it with him.

But in spite of herself, Alice thoughts often turned to Rachel, as did Rachel's unwillingly turned to Alice.

Even before Alice came back to Bay City, Rachel was

haunted by her, nearly thwarted by her.

One afternoon, not long after their return from St. Croix Rachel had stopped in at Steve's office to pick up some credit cards he had taken out for her. While she was there and had his attention she took the opportunity to complain about how Lenore Curtin, Steve's new assistant and an old friend of Alice's, had slighted her at a little get-together the night before.

"She hardly spoke two words to me," Rachel pouted. "I've tried very hard to be friends with Lenore for your sake, Steve."

Rachel had been trying very hard to be friends with Lenore for her own sake for years, and Steve and many others in Bay City knew that, but all he said in reply was, "You don't have to do anything for my sake, Rachel."

That didn't satisfy her. "Well, she works for you, doesn't she?" Several months after the death of her husband, Walter Curtin, Lenore had gone to work for Steve as an administrative assistant in his architectural division. "You'd like us to be friends, wouldn't you?"

"Rachel," Steve said with a sigh. "Lenore and Alice have been bosom buddies since they were kids. You can't expect her not to take Alice's side in all of this."

Rachel stared at Steve in disbelief. "But that means she doesn't approve of what you're doing either."

"That's right."

"Well!" she huffed. "Doesn't that bother you—knowing she doesn't approve?"

He leaned back in his chair. "If I spent my life worrying about whether or not people approved of what I'm doing I'd never get anything done."

Rachel sniffed. "That's easy for you to say. People have to be nice to you, whether they want to or not, and whether they approve of you or not. You're rich, and you're important."

Steve grunted. "Neither of which impresses Lenore."

"Then I don't understand," Rachel said petulantly. "I mean, why does Lenore go on working for you and being your friend? Why doesn't she snub you the way she snubs me?"

His intercom buzzed. Picking up the phone he said into it, "Yes, Pam?"

"Mr. Joe Emery is on line two about your Richfield Housing Project."

"Fine. I'll talk to him." He punched the button for line two, relieved not to have to answer another one of Rachel's silly questions.

During the entire half-hour Rachel stewed about one of her pet peeves, how unfairly people treated her because of Alice.

When the call was finally concluded she had worked herself enough to brave another assault, but this time on new flank. "Steve, can we live in your house out in the country after we're married?"

He was making some notes about his conversation with Joe Emery, and he looked up, frowning. "Why would you want to do that?"

Up went the chin. "Why shouldn't I want to? It's your house, isn't it? It isn't Alice's anymore. And Jamie loves that house. You built the tree house there for him, and he's got that brook to play in in the summertime."

Steve forbore from pointing out that Rachel had refused to allow Jamie to play in either the tree house or the brook while he was married to Alice, except when Alice was on duty at the hospital and therefore nowhere around. Instead, he ignored her, concentrating on his notes.

This habit of letting himself get distracted whenever she tried to talk about anything that mattered to her infuriated Rachel. "Well," she snapped, "why shouldn't we live there?"

Without looking up he replied, "I'm thinking of selling the house."

She stared at him wide-eyed. "You can't do that, Steve. It wouldn't be fair."

That got his attention. "Fair? What does fair have to do with it?"

"Oh, never mind," she said sulkily. "But at least promise me you won't do anything about the house without telling me first."

"All right." The pencil was moving again.

"I mean that, Steve."

He frowned. "I said all right, didn't I? What do you want me to do, Rachel—take an oath in blood?"

"Very funny," she said, and took her new credit cards and left his office, going from there directly to Bryant's Department Store.

Even though Louise Goddard had remained with Eliot Carrington after his separation from Iris—the jet-set Iris having little need for a housekeeper—she was on Iris's payroll as well, and with Iris her loyalties lay.

While Eliot was based in New York, Louise managed to see Iris only on the rare occasions when she stopped in to see Dennis. But now that Eliot and Iris were both in Bay City for the next several months, Louise saw a great deal of her former mistress. And she didn't like what she saw.

The time Iris could spend with her son at Bay City Memorial was limited. Though visiting hours at the hospital were generous, Dennis' drug therapy sessions and their aftermath, his physical therapy, and his tutoring and homework took up most of his waking hours. And Russ was strict about Dennis's physical therapy and his schoolwork.

The time or two Iris had tried to bend the rules only brought her into conflict with Alice and then Russ. So she minded the rules, and as a consequence had a lot of time on her hands.

Getting back in her husband's good graces was one project of these idle hours. On the pretext of wanting to discuss Dennis' condition with him, she tried to arrange to eat dinner with him every night.

Louise Goddard, not unaware of her mistress' intentions, was sitting in the living room of Iris' hotel suite with her, when Eliot called in response to a message Iris had left for him at the desk. Louise squirmed with agitation, when she heard what Iris had to say.

"I know you have work to do, Eliot," she overheard.

"But you do have to eat, don't you? And I do need to talk to you." She glanced apologetically at Louise and made a little face. "Well, all right. Tomorrow night, then." But she was angry when she hung up the phone, slamming it into its cradle.

Louise fretted, "Iris, I wish you wouldn't."

Iris turned to her. "Wouldn't what?"

"Wouldn't make yourself sick over Eliot."

Iris's face reddened. "Whatever makes you say that?"

"It's probably not my place to say it," Louise pursed her lips, "I can't help it. Look at you. You've lost weight, your face is flushed—you're never relaxed—"

"I can't just sit and do nothing," Iris countered, clearly annoyed at the interference.

Maybe not," Louise admitted, "but you *can* take better

78

care of yourself, Iris. Just look at you!"

"There's nothing wrong with me, Louise."

Louise shook her head. "If you go on like this you'll end up in a hospital bed yourself."

"Nonsense. I'm perfectly all right."

"Why are you throwing yourself at Eliot, anyhow? Are you thinking of reconciling with him?"

Iris frowned. "Just because I called to have dinner with him?" But Louise's remark had clearly struck home.

"If it isn't a reconciliation you're after, then why all these phone calls to him to have dinner with you—this isn't the first time, you know—or to go to the hospital to see Dennis with you, or come meet this friend of yours who might be helpful to him on such-and-such a newspaper story?"

"I want to talk to him about Dennis."

"What does the newspaper friend have to do with Dennis?"

"All right. Nothing." Iris raised her hands in surrender. "But I'm not used to being cooped up like this, Louise. I'm only trying to keep busy."

Louise stood up. "Then come for a walk with me along the bay. It's a pretty day out and the exercise will do you good."

"Oh, all right," Iris said.

But it wasn't the exercise alone that did her good. What did give her a boost was running into Rachel.

Iris hadn't called Rachel since her arrival in Bay City. For all Rachel's excuses to her about the disappointing turn of events in St. Croix, Iris was not convinced, and even suspected that, far from trying to throw Alice and Steve together, Rachel had done her best to keep them apart. In addition, Iris found Rachel an unbelievably ignorant social climber of the worst order.

But when she and Louise ran into Rachel on the sidewalk in front of Bryant's Department store Iris, still stinging from Eliot's rebuff, was more than pleased to have a target for her irritation.

"Well, my goodness," Rachel exclaimed. "How nice to see you, Iris." She flashed a bright smile at Louise. "And your friend too." Not waiting for an introduction, she gushed on. "And what a surprise seeing you here. I didn't know anything about it. I mean, you didn't call or anything."

"No, Rachel I didn't. I wasn't sure you'd want to hear from me."

"Why, my goodness, why not?"

"Before I answer that, Rachel, I'd like you to meet my husband's housekeeper—and my friend, Louise Goddard. Louise, this is Rachel Clark. It is still Clark, isn't it, Rachel?"

"Yes. But not for long. Steve and I are getting married just as soon as his divorce from Alice goes through. And I'm sorry, I didn't mean to—how do you do, Mrs. Goddard? It's very nice meeting you."

Louise took Rachel's hand gingerly. "Likewise, I'm sure."

Rachel turned back to Iris. "Why would you think I wouldn't want to hear from you?"

Iris smiled with an almost feline satisfaction. "Because of what I have to tell you, Rachel. My husband is also here in Bay City—"

"Why wouldn't I want to hear that?" Rachel interrupted, puzzled.

"That isn't what I was referring to. Eliot and I are both here because our son is here being treated by Dr. Russell Matthews." She paused dramatically. When Rachel still looked puzzled, she went on, "Well, don't you see? Alice is here too, taking care of Dennis."

The message had finally gotten through. "Alice is here?"

Iris smiled again condescendingly. "Yes. And she'll be here for quite some time to come. Well, Louise, we don't want to keep Rachel standing here. Nice to have seen you. Good-bye, Rachel."

And taking Louise's arm, Iris turned and walked away.

Chapter Five

Sweet Revenge

While Rachel was receiving this unwelcome bit of information from Iris Carrington, John Randolph, who had stopped by Steve's office to bring him the divorce papers he'd drawn up for them, was breaking the news to Steve. "She'll be here only until the boy is able to leave the hospital," John said. "It isn't permanent."

Steve looked up at John from his desk. "Alice has a right to live where ever she wants," he said. "I'm not standing in her way. Or at least I hope I'm not."

John zipped open his briefcase and, taking out the papers, handed them to Steve. "She doesn't want to live here, Steve. There. Look them over when you have the time."

Taking the papers, Steve glanced at them. "Does Alice want to meet with me?"

John shook his head. "No. Emphatically not, I'm afraid."

"Have you worked out a financial settlement?"

"I've suggested one. It's in there."

Steve glanced at the papers again. "I want to give her

enough to make her secure for the rest of her life."

"Look at what I've suggested, and if you think it isn't enough we can sit down together over it. Or maybe you'll want to discuss it with Rachel first."

Steve looked up with one of his smoldering glances. "This is none of Rachel's business. It's mine and Alice's. Or mine anyhow." He stood up. "O.K., John. I know your time is limited. I'll look these over and get back to you."

John zipped the briefcase shut. "How soon are you and Rachel planning to get married?"

Steve shrugged. "As soon as the divorce is final, I guess. Why?"

"Oh, no special reason. But is there any need to rush it?"

"There's no point in delaying it. I should have married Rachel years ago and given my son my name. He'll have it now—and the sooner the better."

John had hardly left his office when he was back again. "I'm sorry," he said. "I could have saved us all some time if I'd had any idea . . . "

Steve had been reading through the divorce papers, and he set them down, not understanding. "Any idea of what?"

John sat himself down, his briefcase on his lap. "Of what Alice's reaction would be. I just ran into her on her lunch break. She says she won't take any financial settlement."

Steve looked exasperated. "Not any at all?"

John shook his head. "No. Not even the one I suggested. She won't take any money from you."

"Well," Steve said wryly. "That's a switch. But then Alice never was interested in my money—unlike some other people I could mention."

"She also wants her maiden name restored."

Steve shook his head. "She must be feeling very bitter toward me."

"Under the circumstances I don't know how you could expect her to feel otherwise," John cautioned.

Steve passed a rough hand through his glossy hair. "I wish somebody would explain those circumstances to me."

It was John's turn show exasperation. "I don't know what needs explaining, Steve. Alice found you with Rachel in the apartment upstairs here—"

Steve sighed. "I could have explained that. Alice could at least have given me the chance."

"I'm afraid," John said, "the time is long since past."

"I know," Steve said with a wave of his hand. "I'm sorry I got into it."

John held out his hand. "If you'll give me those papers, I can make the changes here and now."

Steve passed them to him. "Be my guest."

John took the papers, riffling through them and stopping now and then to scribble in an addition or delete a clause.

"Well," he finally spoke, "this certainly simplifies things. With no property to contest and no offspring"—Steve winced at this—"you'll have your divorce with very little trouble or expense." He shuffled through the papers one last time and handed them back to Steve. "Get these back to me whenever you like. And call me if you have any questions."

For a long time after John left, Steve sat at his desk looking at the stack of papers. The process seemed so orderly and precise, and yet his feelings were so confused and chaotic. Finally Rachel arrived for their lunch date.

With a sigh, he shoved the papers into his briefcase.

"What's that you're working on?" Rachel asked, pointing a well-manicured finger.

"What?" Steve asked distracted. "Oh—John Randolph brought the first draft of the divorce settlement by for me to go over. He says Alice refuses to take any money; she won't even take the house. But that simplifies the proceedings."

Rachel was dumbfounded. To have access to millions and refuse even a dime! She immediately suspected that Alice was up to something. And she wasn't sure she liked the word "simplify," either. But she only said, "Then the house is yours; we can live there after we're married." An idea dawned. "Listen, Steve, that house is *our* house—let's get married there!"

"Where? What are you talking about?" He was so much in the habit of tuning out Rachel's endless chatter that he only half heard her.

"I said, I want us to be married there, I want us to be married on the terrace of your house."

He stared at her in disbelief. "Why on earth—" he said but knowing the answer, said no more.

The chin twitched up. "Because I want to. Because it's your house, and it will be our house—ours and Jamie's. And Jamie can watch the wedding from the tree house you built for him. That way it will be fun for him. We're doing all of this for Jamie, aren't we? So we can be a family together—you and me and him?"

Steve was still staring at her in utter disbelief, but he had found his voice. "No, Rachel," he said, with a shake of his head. "Not the terrace."

As if she had not already gone too far, she went farther. "Why not?" she demanded. "Why not the terrace?

Because it will make you think of Alice? Because it will make you wish you were marrying her again instead of me?"

"No, Rachel, listen—" He felt unusually calm and patient. She was being so preposterous, he realized there was no way to make her understand. And no way to tell her he didn't want to hurt Alice.

But she was standing up and grasping the edge of the desk, knuckles white, a fierce light in her dark eyes. "No. You listen. You can stop everything right now. Your divorce hasn't come to a hearing yet. You're still married to Alice. Well, stay married to her. Tell Jamie you're sorry, but you can't be a real father to him after all. You can only be a part-time father like you have been all along. The only difference is now he'll know you're his father. Now he can see what you're depriving him of."

She straightened up from the desk. "But what difference does it make? Go back to your precious Alice. Forget about me and Jamie."

Steve sat very still, as if he were giving this proposition serious consideration. Then he got up from his desk and strode around it. "Rachel, stop it," he said coldly. "I'm not going back to Alice, and you know it. Look at me. Rachel, I said look at me." His voice was grim, threatening even. "All right. You can have the wedding wherever you want it. Now are you satisfied?"

She hugged his stiff body to her. "Oh, Steve. Oh, thank you. Oh, we'll show them all, we will."

His only answer was to pull away abruptly and dismiss her from the room.

The next afternoon Rachel went to her mother's house to pick up Jamie, where he'd gone after school. Meeting her in the living room, her mother said, "He's playing out back." But when Rachel headed for the kitchen, Ada shot out, "Leave him be a few minutes, Rachel. I want to talk to you."

Rachel turned back startled. "Mom—I haven't got time."

"You're going to take the time." Ada nodded toward the living room sofa. After Rachel had reluctantly sat herself down, Ada continued, "Now what's all this about your being married on the terrace of Steve's house?"

Avoiding her mother's glare, Rachel sniffed, "Well, what about it? Who told you anyhow?"

"Jamie."

"Oh." Rachel shrugged. "Well, it was Steve's idea."

Ada guffawed. "Do you expect me to believe that?"

"I don't care whether you believe it or not. It's true."

"Rachel, don't give me that. Steve may think he doesn't love Alice anymore, but he's not the kind of man to go out of his way to hurt her."

Rachel tossed her dark head. "What difference does it make to Alice where Steve and I get married? She doesn't care anything about him anymore."

Ada shook her head. "I don't believe that. And you don't either. But let's assume it's true. Have you given one thought to what it's going to look like to Alice and her family and her friends if you insist on having your wedding right on the spot where she had hers? Don't you understand how you'll be humiliating her?"

Rachel, who understood that very well, said to her mother, "If you want to read that into it, that's your privilege. But that house belongs to Steve."

Ada grunted. "Courtesy of Alice."

Maybe somewhere deep inside her Rachel realized what

she was doing to herself—and her future in the community—hurting Alice this way. But she gave no sign of it other than the vehemence of her reply. "I don't care courtesy of who," she stormed. "The house belongs to Steve, and he and I are going to live in it, and if we want to get married there, that's our business. If you think I'm going to go through life having to care what Alice or her family or her friends think, then you're mistaken." Pausing angrily for effect, she went on. "The first chance I get, I'm going to do that house over so Steve will forget Alice ever lived there."

Her mother looked at her as much in dismay as in disapproval. "You really think that's going to happen?"

"Yes, I do."

Ada sighed. "Rachel, leave Alice alone."

This unsettled Rachel. "I haven't been anywhere near her. I only found out yesterday she was back."

Ada loved her daughter, but sometimes her crude selfishness was too much. "Rachel, that's not what I'm talking about, and you know it. You're hurting her by doing all these spiteful things. I thought you only wanted to be happy—to be with Steve."

The chin went up again. "I not only want to be, I will be."

Her mother shook her head in resignation. "Not by making Alice miserable you won't. Not by a long shot."

But Rachel had never paid attention to her warnings and today was no different. It sometimes seemed to Ada that Rachel's motivation was closer to self-destruction than selfishness.

As the days preceding the divorce hearing passed, it seemed to Louise Goddard that Iris's pace of living speeded up considerably. Fearful that her former mistress was headed for a nervous breakdown, Louise asked to meet with Eliot for a private talk, in the living room of his hotel suite.

"I'm worried about Iris," she began after Eliot had ushered her to a chair.

"She does seem restless," Eliot agreed, seating himself across from her.

"She's more than restless," Louise confided, "she's ill."

He arched an eyebrow. "Oh, I think you exaggerate, Louise."

"Then you're not paying attention to her."

"I've been forced to pay attention to her, more in the last few weeks than I have in the last two years."

She shook her head. "That's not what I mean."

"Then what do you mean?"

Louise fidgeted in her chair. "I shouldn't have to say this."

Eliot eyed her. "But you're going to."

"I have no choice."

He was becoming impatient. "Then stop beating around the bush, Louise, and say it. You say you think she's ill—in what way?"

"I think she's going to have a nervous breakdown."

"Because of Dennis?" He did not seem taken aback.

Louise glowered at him. "No, not because of Dennis. Because of you. Because of you and Alice."

The light was beginning to dawn. "There is no me and Alice, as you put it."

"Maybe not now. But after her divorce goes through, what's to prevent it?"

Eliot got up from the desk. From one of the windows, he could look down on a small urban park. No more than half a block long, it was worth every inch of its green grass and flowering plants and the small fountain in its center. Eliot could imagine himself sitting quietly, alone on one of the green benches far away from these—complications. "What's to prevent it," he said, turning back to Louise, "are a number of things. For starters, Alice isn't interested in me in any capacity other than friendship."

Louise was stubborn. "With her divorce granted, that could change."

He nodded. "Yes, it could, but even if it did, even if Alice and I both decided we wanted to marry, what could we do about it?"

Louise answered her own question grudgingly. "Iris would have to give you a divorce first."

"Exactly. And what are the chances of that happening?" He waited for her answer. When it didn't come, he prodded, "Well, Louise, aren't you going to answer that?"

She waved a hand. "All right. She's not going to do it."

His case was made, though he had the distinct impression that Louise was just fishing. "Well, there you are. So why should Iris have a nervous breakdown?"

"It isn't just you and Alice, Eliot," she pressed.

"Then what is it?"

Again some moments passed before she answered him. "It's pride, I guess. Having to throw herself at you."

"Have I asked her to throw herself at me?"

"No." Louise gave him a beseeching look. "Eliot, you can't expect logic in something like this."

He made a face. "But I can expect a nervous breakdown, is that it? All right, Louise. Nothing of what we've said so far is anything terribly new. Are you going to tell me there's something I can do to prevent Iris from having a nervous breakdown? Is that what you've been leading up to?" he persisted.

She was squirming again. "I—couldn't you—well, pay more attention to her?" She put a hand up. "I only mean—well, bend a little her way. You do understand that this is a very difficult time for her. Because of Dennis, I mean. Whether she cautions herself against it or not, she has to hope that Dr. Matthews is going to cure Dennis."

Eliot had turned back to the window. "You don't have to lecture me about that, Louise. Don't you think I'm hoping against hope myself? Don't you think that every time I go by that sporting goods store across from the hospital that I have to almost physically restrain myself from going in and buying my son a load of athletic equipment?" He shook his head. "Equipment he dearly wants to use—and may or may not be able to, depending on the outcome of this latest Our-Lady-of-Lourdes approach?" When he once again turned around to Louise she looked pained.

"Don't," she said.

"Then don't you," he countered.

Silence settled around them like dust. Then Eliot crossed the room to his desk. "All right," he said. "Do you know where Iris is?"

"The last I knew she was in her suite."

He picked up his telephone. After a moment he said into it, "Will you connect me with Mrs. Carrington, please . . . Iris? I was wondering if we could have dinner together tonight. No, no special occasion, but now that you say that, wait, I have a better idea. Suppose we meet downstairs at six, go out to the hospital together to see Dennis, and then go on to dinner from there." He listened for a moment or so, frowning at Louise as he did so. "Louise? No, she isn't here. She's out. She said something

at breakfast about going shopping. Why do you ask?"
Another short interval, then, "All right, Iris. Downstairs
at six. I'm looking forward to it."

Cradling the phone, he said to Louise, "There. Now do
you feel better?"

"It's not my feelings I'm concerned about. It's hers."

"I hope she appreciates your concern, Louise."

Louise sometimes wondered if Eliot suspected the
nature—and the depth—of her role as Iris's spy. She tried
not to look flustered as she said, "I'm sure she does. And
thank you for covering for me Eliot. If she knew I'd put
you up to this, that would be worse than your not inviting
her to dinner at all."

Eliot shrugged. "We all have our little secrets, Louise."

He did know, then. She was sure of it. Iris must have
been careless and let something drop.

"Yes, I suppose we do," was her only answer. She left the
suite before anything more could be said.

Early in the week of the divorce hearing, Russ sent for
Alice to come to his office in the hospital. When she
arrived he waved her to a chair and closed the door. "Is it
about Dennis? Has he had some setback?" she queried
him anxiously.

Russ shook his head. "No, it's not about Dennis. It's
about Rachel. I wanted you to hear about it from me—or
at least not from some disinterested bystander."

The anxiety changed to puzzlement. "What's she done
now?"

"It's what she's going to do when she marries Steve."
And he told Alice where the wedding was to be.

Her blue eyes filled with tears. "Oh, how could she?"

Russ put an arm around her. "We both know the

answer to that, Alice, from long experience," he said, handing her his handkerchief to wipe the tears from her eyes.

Alice took it gratefully and wiped her eyes. Stifling a sob, she said, "Well, at least I don't have to be here for it. As soon as the divorce comes through, I'll go back to New York."

"And leave Dennis in somebody else's hands?"

Alice twisted the handkerchief with her thin fingers. "Russ, there are plenty of other nurses who could take care of Dennis . . ."

"Dennis doesn't want plenty of others. He wants you."

"I know, but—" She dabbed at the still flowing tears.

"Alice," Russ said, putting his hands on her arms again, "I shouldn't have brushed aside your 'Oh, how could she' the way I did. Think about it a minute. Why do you think Rachel wants to get married on the terrace?"

"To flaunt herself in front of me. To say, 'Look who I've got'."

"Exactly." He nodded soberly. "And now ask yourself why does she want to do that?"

Alice shook her head forlornly. "I don't know why, Russ."

"Yes, you do. Because she thinks it will accomplish what it is in fact in danger of accomplishing."

Her blue eyes questioned him through the brimming tears.

"Don't you see, Alice? Rachel wants to drive you away, and she thinks humiliating you will do that for her."

For a moment Alice said nothing, then she nodded. "Yes, I suppose you're right."

Russ looked at her intently. "Are you going to let her do that, Alice? *Rachel* of all people? Are you going to let

Rachel dictate to you where you can—or can't—live? Will you let her drive you away from all the people who love you and who want you here in Bay City, to live halfway across the continent?"

Knowing Russ was right, she let his words sink in. After a long pause, "No, I won't let her do it. I'll stay here as long as I'm needed. And if and when I do leave, it will not be because of Rachel, but because of me."

Russ hugged her. "Good girl."

That week Eliot asked Iris to have dinner with him once more, and she accepted as she had the first time, but just as two swallows don't make a summer, two unsought dates with her estranged husband did not make a cure for Iris. The nearer the divorce hearing, the more irrational she became.

The morning after the divorce was granted, she phoned Louise, frightening the housekeeper with her shrill denunciations of Alice, Eliot, and especially Rachel. Thoroughly alarmed now, Louise hastened down to Iris's suite, afraid that she might try to hurt somebody, herself included.

"Who is it?" Iris called from behind the door, answering Louise's knock.

"It's Louise, Iris. Let me in, please."

"No. I've said all I have to say to you."

"Iris, please."

"No."

Louise tried to think what to do. "Do you want me to go get Eliot?"

"No!"

"Then let me in, Iris. Please."

Silence, and then the door opened. Louise slipped

inside before Iris could change her mind.

She was dismayed at what she saw. The living room was in disarray, pillows tossed here, clothes there, and sections of the local newspaper and *The New York Times* scattered about. Iris herself was a mess. It was almost noon and she was still in her light blue satin robe and nightgown. She hadn't so much as brushed her hair, which hung in tangles about her face.

"Iris," she said as gently as she could, "why don't you take a shower and get dressed, and then we'll go have lunch together somewhere."

"I don't want to get dressed," Iris said, her lower lip quivering. "And I'm not hungry."

"Then let me at least brush your hair."

"I don't want you to brush my hair. I just want to be left alone. By you and everybody else." She started toward the door, and Louise thought she was going to ask her to leave, but instead she collapsed into a chair and started weeping. "Oh, it's all her fault."

Louise hurried to her side. "Iris, please."

"I trusted her. She promised me she would help me, and I trusted her."

Louise thought privately that anybody who trusted Rachel to do anything except advance herself needed to have her head examined, but she said nothing. Comforting Iris for a few moments, the angular housekeeper went into the bathroom and took two tablets from their vial, filled a glass with water, and came back into the living room. "Here," she said, holding glass and tablets out to Iris. "Take these. It will make you feel better." On one of her visits to Russ Matthews to ask about his progress with Dennis, Iris had complained to the doctor that she was having trouble sleeping, and he had prescribed some sedatives for her. Louise didn't approve of drugs, especially drugs a person could get addicted to, but right now she thought anything was better than to let Iris carry on this way.

The distraught woman pushed them away. "I don't want to feel better. I want to let Rachel know how I feel about her."

Louise felt this was probably not a good idea. On the other hand, maybe releasing her pentup hostilities would be the end of it.

"Do you want me to get her on the phone for you?" she asked.

"Yes," Iris responded. But as Louise headed for the phone, she thought better of it. "No, wait. I'll go see her in person, talk to her."

Louise half-heartedly tried to dissuade her, but Iris was adamant. So she merely sat and waited while Iris showered and dressed. Appearance had always mattered a great deal to Iris, and Louise clung to the notion that once she was properly dressed, her sense of propriety would return as well.

When Iris emerged from her bedroom half an hour later, she didn't look her best—her shoes didn't match her dress, and her purse didn't go with either—but she looked better than she had.

Louise held out her hand. "You can't go like that," she said appeasingly. "Let me get another purse for you."

As Iris snatched her purse away from Louise's outstretched hand, two vivid spots of color sprang to her face. "No, you don't," she said wildly. "And don't you try to stop me, Louise, or I'll use them on you as well."

Louise felt giddy with confusion. "I don't know what you're talking about. Use what on me?"

Iris dug in the purse and pulled out a pair of scissors, thrusting them at Louise. "We'll see what Rachel says when she sees these."

Without thinking, Louise lunged at her employer, wrested the scissors out of her grasp, and flung them across the room. "Are you mad?" she exclaimed, pushing Iris down into a chair. "Do you want to go to jail?"

Iris stared at her incoherently, then burst into tears again, her body sagging in defeat. "Everybody is against me," she wailed.

Louise felt the time had come for her take charge. She once again held out the sedatives and the glass of water to her. "Take these."

"I don't want them," Iris said through her tears.

"I don't care if you don't want them, Iris. I said take them."

Exhaustion and emotion has taken their toll. Iris finally submitted without a murmur.

"And listen to me," Louise went on. "Rachel doesn't need you to destroy her. Rachel doesn't need anybody to do it. Given enough time with Steve Frame she'll destroy herself, and drive him back into Alice Matthews' arms. Then all your worries will be over. Do you hear me, Iris?"

Iris nodded vacantly. "Yes, I hear you." The haughty movie star visage was almost unrecognizable now.

"And do you understand me?"

"I guess so, Louise."

"All right. Now you just sit there and let the medicine calm you down. Have you had anything to eat today?"

"No."

Louise went to the phone and ordered orange juice, toast and coffee from room service. While she waited, she bustled about, tidying the room, taking special care to hide the scissors. After breakfast, she sat with Iris until the pills—and the food, too—did their work. By the time Iris was asleep, Louise had made up her mind to speak to Eliot again.

On June fifteenth, only a few days after the divorce was granted, Steve Frame and Rachel were married on the terrace where he and Alice had been married scarcely two years before. Right up until the day of the ceremony various people had tried to talk Rachel into changing the location. Not only did she pay no attention to them, she did one more thing to humiliate Alice—she insisted she and Steve fly to St. Croix to his house there for their honeymoon.

Rachel thought life was perfect now that she, not Alice, was Mrs. Steven Frame.

Even so, Alice continued to haunt her. The newlyweds hadn't been back from St. Croix more than a few days when they had their first quarrel—over Alice.

Chapter Six
Quiet Desperation

Louise wasted no time in following through on her decision to speak to Eliot. He was able to meet with her that same day.

She knocked on his door at the appointed hour, and entered when he spoke up. Before sitting down she said, "Are you working against a deadline?"

He shook his head. "Not really. No. Sit down, Louise. Actually I'm ahead of schedule."

Taking a chair, she smoothed her skirt and cleared her throat. "I want to talk to you about Iris."

"I see. Well." Involuntarily, his eyes flicked to his watch. "What is it this time?"

"She's having the nervous breakdown I warned you against." She told him what had happened earlier, gratified by the look of alarm that filled his face.

"Who's with her now?" he asked, about to leap to his feet.

Louise put up a hand. "One of the hotel maids is with her. Iris is sleeping now. And I told the girl I'd only be a few minutes."

Eliot frowned. "Shouldn't we get her to a hospital—or a sanitarium of some kind? There must be some facility here in Bay City for this kind of thing." He reached for the telephone book.

"I think she needs to see a doctor, yes," Louise agreed. "Maybe Dr. Matthews can recommend somebody. But I don't think—I mean, the reason I wanted to talk to you, Eliot—other than to tell you what happened—is to suggest—well, that I quit as your housekeeper and go take care of Iris."

He had been leafing through the phone book. Now he put it aside, and folded his long, thin fingers over each other.

"You don't really need me here in Bay City," Louise went on. "Most of the time I'm sitting around trying to come up with something to keep me busy. And now Iris is going to have to have somebody with her full time."

Eliot considered this and nodded. "Yes, I agree with you."

"And when you go back to New York—well, we can see what the situation is then . . ."

"All right, Louise. Have you spoken to Iris?"

"No. I wanted to speak to you first. But I'm sure it will be all right with her. I don't see that we have any other choice."

For the next few days, Iris was alternately withdrawn and sullen, to the extent that neither Louise nor Eliot was certain that she knew about the arrangement they had agreed upon. Nor did she know that Louise consulted with Russ Matthews about recommending a psychiatrist for her. The psychiatrist, a young man named Richard Bollings who had gone to medical school with Russ, came to Iris's hotel suite, talked to Eliot and Louise, then closeted himself with Iris in her bedroom for a private interview.

Emerging from the interview, he told Eliot and Louise, "I'm going to prescribe some medication to get her on an even keel emotionally first. I'll put her on my regular appointment schedule, but if she is to stay here, I'll want her to have nursing care around the clock."

"But Dr. Bollings—" Louise began.

He put up a hand. "I know what you're going to say, Mrs. Goddard. You've already said it. You'll be here yourself to take care of Mrs. Carrington."

"Yes," she said. "I don't need any outside help."

"On the contrary," Dr. Bollings said. "You can't maintain a twenty-four-hour vigil without risking your own collapse. No, Mrs. Goddard, nursing care around the clock. Either that or I put her in a clinic."

Eliot turned to her. "Dr. Bollings makes the decisions, Louise."

"All right," she said. She had harbored hope, faint though it was, that she and Eliot could divide up the twenty-four-hour vigil, thus bringing him back into Iris's life in a meaningful way, but Louise, having learned long ago to adapt and adjust, never held out for impossible goals. She would do what the doctor ordered, and when Iris was improved enough to know what was happening, they would put their heads together and figure out some other way to keep Eliot from straying.

"One other thing," Dr. Bollings was saying, "though I'm sure I don't have to remind you of it. Russ—Dr. Matthews is concerned about the effect his mother's illness may have on Dennis. Until she is well enough to resume visiting him, we're going to tell him she's down with the flu, and doesn't want to risk passing it on to him. All right?"

Eliot and Louise both nodded.

"I realize," he said, "that June is not exactly flu season. Still, these things happen, and I doubt that Dennis will question it."

The boy didn't, of course, and to compensate, Eliot increased his own visits, giving him encouraging reports about his mother's progress until Iris was well enough first to talk to her son by phone and then to visit him in person, accompanied by Louise.

Under Dr. Bolling's medication, Iris could almost have been described as docile. The one thing that bothered her about having Louise in her open employ, and having her there full-time, was she no longer had access to information about Eliot. She stewed about that until she came up with a solution.

"I don't know why I didn't think of it sooner," she said triumphantly to Louise one morning at the breakfast table. Handing her the front section of *The New York Times* she went on, "Look at that article midway down the page. There's our answer."

The article was about electronic bugging. Louise read enough to satisfy Iris, but she was dubious about such activity and said so. "What if he finds out?"

Iris was wearing her light blue satin dressing gown, but her hair was brushed, and her face carefully made up. Nobody looking at her would know there was anything wrong. "If we find somebody who's a real professional, and he does a professional job of it, why should Eliot even suspect anything, let alone find out about it?"

"I suppose you're right."

"Of course I am. Get me the telephone book, Louise."

As Louise got up to retrieve it, she said to herself that nobody listening to Iris give orders would suspect that anything was amiss either. She was her old imperious self. Returning with the phone book, Louise gave it to her mistress and sat down to finish her breakfast.

Iris looked at listings. "The trouble is," she complained, "just because somebody claims he's an expert doesn't mean he is. And nobody's going to admit to being anything less than perfect." She put the phone book aside and got up from the table. "I have a better idea."

Louise looked up from her toast and coffee. "Where are you going?"

"To call a friend of mine in Chicago. He'll know somebody."

She returned elated. "A man will be here tomorrow afternoon. All we have to do is get Eliot out of his suite for a couple of hours."

They didn't even have to arrange that. The words were hardly out of Iris's mouth when the phone rang. It was Eliot, saying he had to fly to San Francisco for a couple of days. He'd be at the Mark Hopkins if they had to get in touch with him. Otherwise he'd call when he got back.

Iris clapped her hands, beaming. "Perfect," she chortled. "Perfect."

The next afternoon the man came in from Chicago and bugged Eliot's suite, except for the bedroom that would be Dennis's when he was discharged from the hospital. Then the electronics expert showed Louise how to remove the reels from the tape recorder he installed in their suite. After she had transcribed what was on them, she could erase them and reinstall them. "Unless," he said, "you want to send them out to a public stenographer."

Louise shook her head emphatically. "No. I can do them myself." She had often done typing for Eliot, and much of that had been transcriptions of recorded interviews. This task would be quite simple.

"Well," the man said, "if you have any problems, this is where you can reach me." He handed Louise his business card. As if to distance herself from this unsavory business, Iris had stayed in the background.

Showing the man out Louise thought to herself that, to paraphrase Émile Coué, day by day, and in every way, Iris was getting better and better.

When Steve married Alice they honeymooned at his house in St. Croix for several months. By contrast, his honeymoon there with Rachel lasted a little less than three weeks. Maybe that was what motivated her to act as she did on their return to Bay City.

In the course of having the house redecorated Rachel came across a yellow baby bunting. One afternoon when Steve's sister Janice was at the house with her, she showed it to her. "I suppose it was for Alice's baby," she said. "You know. The one she lost."

"Yes," Janice agreed. "I suppose it was. What are you going to do with it?"

"I don't know, but I'm sure I can find some use for it."

What she did was send it to Alice, along with a note saying she had found it and thought Alice probably wanted it back.

For a few days there was no reaction as far as Rachel knew. The climax to this bit of spite came at—and after—a party Steve gave to introduce Pat and John Randolph to his sister Janice. Pat was standing at the door to the terrace, a little apart from the others, when Rachel came over to her. Pat gave her a polite smile—the most she could muster. "How are you, Rachel?"

The cordiality was returned with venom. "I'm a lot

better off than you ever expected to see me. Isn't that right?"

Pat drew herself up. "I'm sorry, Rachel. I was only trying to be friendly."

Rachel didn't give ground. "Trying or pretending? You don't need to pretend to be friendly to me, Pat. I know how you feel about me, how you've always felt about me—you and the rest of your family."

Somebody had once said that *Pat* was short for *patrician*, and that perfectly described Alice's sister: tall, slender, elegant, a beautiful blonde with fine, even features—and a manner to match. She said now, as evenly as she could, "Do you think this is the time or the place for this sort of thing?"

"I wouldn't know," Rachel snapped at her. "I didn't have the social upbringing all you Matthewses had." She snorted. "It must gall you to know you have to be nice to me."

The edge in Pat's voice hardened to ice. "I don't have to be anything to you, Rachel. Nice or not."

"Oh, yes, you do," Rachel needled, "if you want to keep Steve's business. And of course you do want to keep it, because if John didn't have Steve's legal business, he wouldn't have any business at all."

Pat fixed a cold stare on her. "I didn't know you were such an expert on legal affairs, Rachel. But then, with all your other intellectual accomplishments, I should have expected it."

That hit home, as Pat had intended. Rachel turned red. "I accomplished one thing you never thought I could."

"That's right," Pat agreed. "You have. I have to admit I don't understand it. I like Steve, and I think he deserves the best there is, but then . . ." Leaving the sentence unfinished, she turned and walked away.

After the party was over and everybody had gone, Steve and Rachel were collecting glasses and ashtrays, when he said to her, "What were you and Pat having words about earlier tonight?"

"We weren't 'having words' about anything," Rachel sniffed. "I was only trying to be nice to her."

He grunted. "The same way you were trying to be nice to Alice a couple of weeks ago when you sent that baby outfit to her?"

Rachel dropped the glass she was holding, and it shattered on the bare floor. Stooping to pick up the pieces Rachel said, "Who told you that?"

He made no attempt to help her but went on with his own cleaning up. "Does it matter who told me?"

"I suppose it was Pat. It sounds like her."

"No, it wasn't Pat. It was Lenore. But that's beside the point." He stood looking down at her. "Why did you do it, Rachel?"

She stared up at him, then looked away. "Well, I don't know why you're looking at me like that. I didn't do it to upset her."

Steve shook his head. "What other possible effect could it have on her? It was a cruel, malicious thing to do."

Rachel gathered the broken pieces of glass and dumped them in a wastebasket. "You're reading something into it I didn't intend. The bunting belonged to Alice. I was just returning it to her."

"Because she had some use for it?"

Rachel spun around to him. "Because I don't want anything of Alice's in this house. Why do you think I had the house redecorated? Did you think I wanted to be reminded of Alice every minute of every day I live here?"

Steve hadn't taken his eyes off her face. "Did you think Alice wanted to be reminded of the baby she wanted so much and lost?"

"Oh," Rachel said, turning away from him again, "you're making a mountain out of a molehill."

Steve put his hand out and, grabbing her wrists, turned her toward him. "I want you to write Alice a note, Rachel."

"I already wrote her one when I sent her the baby bunting."

"I'm talking about an apology."

She stood there glaring at him, clenching and unclenching her pinioned hands. Finally she twisted away from him. "Oh, all right."

When they had finished the job of clearing away the party debris, she said, "Are you coming upstairs with me?"

He shook his head. "No. You go on. I'll be up later." He did not seem remorseful or even angry as Rachel watched him walk back into the living room and throw himself on the sofa. But her heart sank as he sat before the empty fireplace, staring into it. Slowly she turned and went up to bed alone.

A few days later, knowing that Steve was out of town on business, Rachel went to his office to see Lenore. Leading the way into an empty conference room, Lenore asked, "What is it, Rachel?"

Closing the door, Rachel sat down at the large round table a few places away from Lenore. With a toss of her pretty head, she challenged, "If you don't want to like me or be friends with me, Lenore—well, that's your business, I guess—even though you do work for my husband."

"Please get to the point, Rachel," she said.

"I'm getting there. What I want is for you to stop

making trouble between Steve and me. You told him I sent that baby bunting to Alice."

"If anybody is making trouble between you and Steve, Rachel, it's you, not me," Lenore pointed out.

Then the chin went up. "You had no business telling him."

"You had no business doing it. Nobody except Steve can keep you from doing the things you do, Rachel. That's why I told him. I can't stand by and let you go on hurting Alice the way you have been."

Rachel pounded her fist on the conference table. "Oh, Alice, Alice, Alice. I'm sick to death of hearing about Alice all the time."

"You wouldn't keep hearing about her," Lenore said, "if you'd only leave her alone."

"I haven't done anything to her."

"You married her husband in her house for starters."

"It isn't Alice's house. It's Steve's. And mine."

"It was built for Alice."

Rachel made a face. "Well, she didn't want it."

"She certainly didn't want you to be married in it or live in it, to taunt her the way you do. Can't you be satisfied with what you have, Rachel? Do you have to make Alice miserable in order to be happy?"

"I have a right to live in that house," Rachel stormed, "and I intend to go on living in it."

"And do you intend to find other ways to torment Alice—to drive her out of Bay City?"

Lenore had articulated Rachel's deepest desire. Glaring at Lenore, she said, "I'd do more than that if I could."

Lenore pushed back from the table and, walked to the door of the conference room. Opening it, she said, "Get out, Rachel."

Rachel finally knew the flush of pleasure she had longed for, the long sought exercise of power. "I'll have you know this is my husband's property, not yours."

The gleam of triumph in Rachel's eyes disgusted Lenore. "Then sit there and make the most of it, Rachel. While you can." And with that, she left the conference room.

Rachel's moment of glory, though, was quickly followed by anxiety. She remained for some time where she was, not to prove anything to Lenore, but because the exchange—and all its implied threats—had left her shaken. Usually the most kindhearted of people, even to those she didn't like, Lenore had not minced words with Rachel; Rachel suspected she did not mince them with Steve, either.

The night Steve was expected home from his business trip, Rachel showered and dressed in one of her prettiest outfits, a pale-green silk chiffon, with clingy lines and a low neckline. She looked through their collection of records, choosing some of the most romantic melodies to put on the stereo, and started up the turntable when she saw his car pull into the circular driveway in front of the house.

She was at the door to meet him, martini in each hand. "Welcome home, darling," she said after he gave her a somewhat perfunctory kiss at the door. Setting his briefcase down, he took the martini she offered him and sat down on the sofa.

"I have something to show you," she said. Going to the table that stood by the wall alongside the fireplace, she picked up an envelope and handed it to him. "Read it. It's my apology to Alice."

He extracted the note, read it, and handed it back to

her. "It's a nice note, Rachel."

She sighed. "I was hoping that's what you'd say, Steve. I really worked on it."

He took a sip of his martini. "Yes, I'm sure you did."

Nervously Rachel put the note aside and came back to sit beside Steve on the sofa. "Do you forgive me, Steve?"

"It's for Alice, not for me, to forgive you, Rachel. She's the one you hurt."

Rachel felt her temper heating up, but told herself to watch what she said. Taking her cue from his response she said, "Everybody cares about how much Alice has been hurt. Nobody even thinks about my side of it—how hard it is for me to try to take her place, how hard it is for me to try to make you happy, Steve, when I know you're constantly comparing me to her."

Steve frowned at Rachel over the rim of his martini. "I'm not constantly comparing you to her."

"But you do think about her."

Steve put his drink down on the table in front of the sofa. "All right, Rachel, yes. Of course I think about her. You can't wipe a person out of your mind by simply deciding you won't think about her. It isn't that easy."

Beyond the less-than-satisfying kiss at the door, Steve had made no move to display any affection toward her, not even so much as a touch, despite her very physical closeness to him there on the sofa. Not sure what to do next, Rachel got up and moved to stand in front of him. Waving a hand at the room around them, she said, "And you see Alice here—in this house—in spite of all my redecorating, don't you?"

"Yes, Rachel, that too." He sat looking up at her with his dark, brooding eyes. She had never been much good at perceiving what he was thinking or feeling, and she couldn't tell now. "But it wasn't my idea to live here, remember," he continued. "I wanted to sell this house."

She nodded contritely. "I know you did. I'm sorry now I talked you out of it."

Rachel had only two weapons to draw on in her effort to win Steve to her. One was their son, Jamie; the other was her sex appeal. Desperate now to keep Lenore's warnings from coming true, she tried using both. Moving back to the sofa, she sat down beside him again and clutched his hand in hers. "Oh, Steve," she begged, "please help me. I don't want to lose you. I'm so afraid I will, and what will become of Jamie and me then?"

Steve didn't take his hand away, but neither did he make any move toward her. "Why don't you think of that before you do the things you do?" he asked.

She raised his hand and pressed it to her lips. "Please don't make things any harder for me than they are already."

At that, he pulled his hand away from her. "Rachel," he said, "we agreed when we got married—before we got married—that we'd be honest and open with each other. I've tried to hold up my end of the bargain, but I don't think you have."

Her instinct was to deny that, but she knew he was speaking the truth. "I will from now on, Steve. I promise."

"What gives your promise more value this time than last?" His eyes had darkened.

Clasping her hands together, she made herself sound as earnest as she could. "Because I've seen what not keeping the promise does." She reached out as if to take his hand again in hers, but stopped. "Steve, please. One thing we've always had in common, you and I, is knowing we're not perfect. We know we're going to make mistakes. We know we're going to do things other people don't approve of. But can't we learn from our mistakes?"

Though she was sitting as close to him as she could without actually touching him, he edged away from her. "That's a question you'd be better off asking yourself, Rachel, instead of me."

"All right," she said, giving in. "I can learn, and I will. Oh, Steve, if you knew how much I love you. If you knew how much it's meant to Jamie having the three of us together as a family."

Steve shot her a skeptical look. "If it means so much to Jamie, why did you pack him off to his grandmother's tonight?"

"I didn't pack him off," she said, already, with those few words, breaking her heartfelt promise to be honest with him. "Mom misses not seeing as much of him as she used to, when we lived in town. And he misses her. Besides, I didn't know what time you'd be getting back tonight until you called me from the office, whether it would be before his bedtime or after."

"All right," he said, in no mood to argue. "I'm sorry. I'm not at my best tonight."

She was instantly solicitous. "Was your business trip a rough one?"

"It was tiring."

She reached for his martini glass. "Let me fix you another drink."

"No, thanks, Rachel, I don't want another one. I can't even finish this one."

She stood up and pirouetted for him. "Do you like my dress, Steve?"

"It's very pretty, yes."

She sat down beside him again, snuggling as close as she

dared. "I wish I'd thought to meet you in town when you came home tonight." She squeezed his arm affectionately.

He blinked. "Why?"

She shrugged as prettily as she could. "We could have spent the night in your bachelor apartment. Above your office." She tried a smile. "Do you remember the first time I spent the night with you?"

He edged away from her again. "I'm not likely ever to forget that."

"The last time I was there with you, you said you weren't sorry I'd stayed. Do you remember that?"

He nodded. "Yes, Rachel. I remember."

"Steve," she said thrusting herself at him, "kiss me. Please."

He patted her hand, then stood up from the sofa. "I'm sorry, Rachel. I'm tired. Some other time."

"But, Steve—" she said, catching at him.

He pulled away. "I said some other time, Rachel. I've had two days of nonstop negotiations, and I'm dead on my feet. With two sips of that martini I knew I was finished." He yawned and stretched, then went to check the thermostat of the air conditioner. Turning it up a bit, he said, "I'm going on upstairs to try to get some sleep. I'll see you in the morning."

In disbelief, she watched him go.

He had never before failed to respond to her attempts to seduce him—except maybe a few times when he'd been married to Alice and she tried making him see what a mistake he'd made.

When he disappeared from view, she swept over to the table and picked up her note of apology to Alice, intending to tear it up. But thinking better of it, she got herself under control—tearing up the note would only make matters worse for her. No, she would go ahead and mail the stupid thing off to Alice.

She turned off the stereo—a fat lot of good it had done her—and sat down to watch some television. Not much was on that she hadn't already seen last winter, but it was either watch a rerun or the Detroit Tigers. She settled for the rerun, telling herself tomorrow would be better.

She was wrong about that. Tomorrow was even worse.

Chapter Seven

Trapped

The next morning, about an hour after Steve had left for the office, the front doorbell rang. Going to answer it, wondering who it could be, Rachel was surprised—and not altogether pleased—to see her father standing on the front porch.

"Well, Rachel, honey," said Gerald Davis, his arms outstretched to her, "here's your old man back in town."

"Yes," she said, accepting his embrace, "so I see. Well." She held the door for him. "Come in. Have you come to visit us?"

He followed her inside. "I don't know. It all depends. I might move back here permanently."

Rachel was fond of her father, and there were even times when she was more than fond of him. But she knew Steve didn't like him, and now that her own position with Steve seemed so precarious, her father was more of a threat than a comfort. "What happened to your job in San Francisco?" she asked.

A silly, apologetic grin spread across her father's face. "I lost it. And I lost what money I had on the way here, in

Vegas." He shrugged nonchalantly.

"Well," she said doubtfully, "I suppose you can stay here with us."

"No, I don't need that. I've got a place to stay in town." Rachel breathed a little easier.

"All I'm asking, Rachel, is a chance to talk with Steve."

That was the last thing she wanted to hear from him. Frowning, she said, "What good would that do, Dad? Steve doesn't know anything about the restaurant business. You don't know how relieved he was to finally get The Hearthside Inn off his hands."

"I'm not asking about the restaurant business. All I want is a little help, and that he *can* give me. He should give it to me. He owes it to me."

The faint feeling of dread that had begun to seep through Rachel at sight of her father on the front porch now turned to alarm. "You mean," she said, "because of what you did for Steve and me?"

"That's right."

The color drained out of her face. "But you can't tell him about that, Dad! You can't! It would be the end of everything for me."

Her father put an arm around her and hugged her to him. "Don't worry, honey. I'm not going to tell him anything. Trust me. Just set up an appointment for me with him, will you?"

"All right," she said. But she said it reluctantly, and it was on reluctant feet that she went to the telephone to call Steve, whose voice matched her feelings when he agreed to meet with his father-in-law later that morning.

When Gerald arrived to keep the appointment, Steve did not get up from his desk to welcome him but merely waved him to a chair and said brusquely, "Sit down,

Gerald." His lack of interest was quite obvious.

Gerald sat. "Well," he said, smiling, "you're looking good, Steve. The world treating you all right?"

Steve did not smile in return. In that same brusque voice he said, "Rachel said you wanted to see me."

"That's right." He leaned forward confiding. "I had what you might call a difference of opinion with the restaurant owner out in San Francisco. I suppose it was inevitable. I'm not used to working for somebody else, you see. I like working for myself." He put on another smile and sat back in the chair. "That's were you come in."

Steve did not find any of that amusing. "In what way?"

Gerald was feeling the chill emanating from Steve's side of the desk—and feeling less sure of himself. "All right," he said in a getting-down-to-business manner. "I know you've got other things to do. I won't waste any more of your time. I want you to set me up in business. In the restaurant business, since that's what I know best."

Steve was already shaking his head. "I'm afraid not."

Gerald stared at him, stung. "Just like that?" he asked. "You're not even willing to hear what I have to say?"

"That's right," Steve replied, mimicking Davis's confidential manner. "I want no part of any business deal with you, Gerald. I had enough of you the last time around." He stood up, signaling the end of the interview.

Gerald stood too, but he made no move to go. "You owe it to me, Steve."

"I owe you nothing. The money you invested in The Hearthside Inn was repaid to you in full."

"I'm not talking about money. I'm talking about Rachel."

Steve shook his head again. "If you think I owe you any obligation as Rachel's father, think again. Her mother, yes. If Ada came to me for help, I'd give it to her. But what have you ever done for Rachel except walk out on her?"

"If it weren't for me," Gerald blurted out, "you wouldn't be married to Rachel."

"That's a lot of hot air." Steve started around his desk. "Now, as you pointed out yourself a couple of minutes ago, I do have other business to attend to. So if you don't mind . . ."

Gerald stood his ground. "You think it was an accident Alice found you and Rachel together that night in your apartment over this office?"

Steve stopped in his tracks and stared at the older man. "What are you talking about?"

"I'm talking about the night Alice left you—and why she left. Because she found you and Rachel all cozied up together."

For a moment Gerald thought Steve was going to hit him. "That's a lie!" he shouted. "Rachel and I were not cozied up together."

"You were together."

"Yes. To talk about Jamie." A purple vein in Steve's temple was throbbing wildly.

"Whatever. Anyway, Alice found you there. Well, I'm the one who called the hospital and left a message for Alice to go to your office so she *would* find you there with Rachel. With Alice out of the way, I knew it was only a question of time before you turned to Rachel. And I was right, wasn't I? Now you still say you owe me nothing?"

Steve was frozen to the spot he stood on, the color draining out of his face. "You did that? You and Rachel?"

Mesmerized by the throbbing vein, Gerald shook his head. "No. Rachel had nothing to do with it. She didn't even know about it at the time." He drew back involuntarily from the look in Steve's eyes. "I swear she didn't."

"I don't believe you."

Gerald began to feel alarmed. "It's the truth, Steve. I didn't tell Rachel anything about it until just before I left Bay City last March. And that was months after Alice left you. Rachel had nothing to do with it."

Steve strode to the door and opened it. "Get out of my office."

"Steve, you're a happy man now, aren't—"

"Get out."

"Steve, look—" But the look in Steve's eyes shut him up. He put up a hand as if in self-defense. "All right. I'm going. I'm sorry you—oh, never mind." And he got out.

From Steve's office Gerald drove his rental car back out to the house in the country.

"Well?" Rachel said at the door, not bothering with the amenities, "how did things go with Steve?"

Gerald looked sheepish. "Aren't you even going to ask me in for a cup of coffee?"

"All right. Come in." She opened the door just wide enough for him to pass through. She had just brewed up some coffee, and poured out a cup for each of them. "Well?" she repeated dully.

Her father hunched his shoulders. "Things didn't go so well. Right from the minute I walked into his office he suspected that I knew something about that night. When Alice found you with Steve, I mean."

Rachel waved an impatient hand. Things were taking a very unpleasant turn. "I know what night you're talking about, Dad. What do you mean, he suspected?"

"Just what I said. He began bombarding me with questions about where I was and what was I doing, until

119

he tripped me up and forced the whole story out of me."

Rachel's jaw dropped. "I don't believe you."

Her father avoided her stare. "He didn't either, I don't think, when I told him you'd had no part in it. A fine thing," he went on, ignoring the furious look on his daughter's face, "I do you a big favor and what I think is a big favor for Steve, and the upshot is I'm out with him."

Rachel could no longer contain herself. *"You're* out with him!" she screamed at her father. "What about me?" She buried her face in her hands. "Oh, why did you ever do such a dumb thing in the first place?"

"If I hadn't," Gerald said, getting to his feet, his coffee still untouched, "you'd still be married to that loser, Ted Clark. No, don't get up Rachel. I don't need to get thrown out twice in one morning."

He left her sitting there, staring into her now cold cup of coffee.

After Gerald Davis left the office, Steve went back to his desk trying to absorb what he had just been told. Then he picked up his phone and called Eliot Carrington's hotel suite. When Carrington answered, Steve asked to speak to Alice.

"May I tell her who's calling?"

"Yes," Steve replied. "Tell her It's Steve Frame."

"Just a moment, please. I'll see if she'll talk to you." There was a click and a silence as Eliot put him on hold, and then his voice came on the line again. "I'm sorry, Steve. She's not available right now."

Steve sighed. "Will you ask her to call me then, please? I'm at the office. She knows the number."

"I'll give her the message."

For all the good it will probably do, Steve thought, as he hung up. The rest of that morning and throughout the day, each time his intercom buzzed, he picked up his phone, his heart in his mouth, but it was never Alice.

He hadn't really expected it would be.

Alice had been helping Dennis with some school work when Steve's call came through. Even though it was August, a time when most kids were on vacation, Dennis had so much catching up to do he'd been tutored all summer long and was preparing for the teacher's arrival.

When the man came, punctually at eleven, Alice left them in Dennis' room and settled herself in the living room with a lapboard, intending to write some letters. She'd only been at it a few minutes when Eliot came out of his study.

"Did you return Steve's call?" he asked.

She shook her head. "No."

Eliot studied her a few moments. "Are you going to?"

"No, I don't think so, Eliot."

"Because it's too painful for you?"

"That's one reason . . ." Her voice trailed off.

"Do you have any idea what he wants?"

"No. Well—some idea, I suppose, yes. I suppose he wants to talk about my leaving him. Why I did it. Though why it should still matter to him, I don't know—now that he's married to Rachel, I mean."

"Maybe the marriage isn't working out."

"Maybe it isn't," Alice agreed. "My sister Pat once said—oh, well." The agitation that set her pulse racing earlier had left her drawn and exhausted. "Never mind what she said. What can that matter anymore?"

Eliot sat across from her, his elbows on his knees, watching her pensively. "What did your sister say?"

"She said Rachel always wants what she can't have, and then when she gets it, she can't cope." Alice frowned down at the lapboard. "Pat said wait and see. Rachel will end up destroying her own happiness the way she—" Alice swallowed a few times. "The way she destroyed our happiness. Steven's and mine."

Again Eliot was silent as if trying to decide what to say. "I'm sorry for bringing the whole business up, Alice. I shouldn't have. I don't mean to cause you pain."

She managed a bleary smile. "It's all right, Eliot. I know you don't. And it's better to talk about it than bottling it all up inside. Or at least I think it's better." She gave a little shrug. "Sometimes I think I don't know my own mind. Or heart."

"Then maybe you should return his call. At least find out what he wants."

She didn't respond immediately, a sign to Eliot that she was wavering. But when she did answer, it was with a shake of her blond head. "No, I don't think so, Eliot. It may have been something he did on impulse. Something he already regrets doing."

Eliot shook his head. "If it's something he regrets doing he only has to pick up the phone and call again to cancel the message."

Alice nodded. "Yes. I know that."

"I haven't heard the phone ring."

"No. Neither have I."

Again a silence.

"Well?" he said at last.

But still she refused. "No, I don't think so. But thanks for being interested, Eliot."

"I've told you before, Alice if there's anything I can do to help make things better for you, I'll do it. Anything."

"I know. And I appreciate it, Eliot, more than maybe you realize."

Then, with a shake of his head, Eliot rose and went back to his room.

Each day at noon and again at the end of the day Louise Goddard checked the reels of tape from the bugging of Eliot's hotel suite to see what, if anything, was on them. Less than an hour after Eliot's talk with Alice about whether or not she would return Steve's phone call, Louise had transcribed the entire conversation. Checking through the typescript to look for errors, finding none, she clipped the pages together and slipped them into a manila folder.

Iris was having a glass of tomato juice in the living room of her suite while waiting for room service to send lunch up. When Louise came in Iris looked up and said, "Just because Dr. Bollings won't permit me to have any wine doesn't mean you can't have any, Louise."

Louise shook her head. "I don't want any, Iris."

Iris wrinkled her nose. "You mean you prefer this boring tomato juice?"

"No. I don't want any of that either. Here, I have something for you." She took the papers out of the folder and handed them to Iris.

At the sight of Alice's name, Iris perked up. "Is this something good?"

Louise nodded. "I think so, yes. Read it all, and then we can talk about it."

Iris set down the glass of tomato juice and read the transcription from start to finish. "Well!" she exclaimed when she had finished. "I think you're right. Except for this last part. I don't much care for that."

Louise peered over her shoulder. "What part is that?"

Iris ran her eyes down the page. "Where Eliot says, 'I've told you before Alice, if there's anything I can do to help make things better for you, I'll do it. Anything.' I don't like the way he says that." Iris shook her sleekly coiffed blond head. "Or Alice's answer either." She read from the transcript again. "'I know. And I appreciate it, Eliot, more than maybe you realize.'" Iris chewed her lip. "And then the silence afterward. Do you think he kissed her?"

Louise frowned. "I don't think so, Iris. Surely the tape would have given us some indication of something like that."

That calmed her a little. "Yes. I suppose you're right." She read through the transcript again, from start to finish, and then looked over at Louise seated in a chair across from her. "Do you think Alice will return Steve's call?"

Louise's angular body shifted slightly in her chair. "I don't know, but judging from the tone of her voice, I think she's tempted. Doesn't it sound like that to you, even in this typed version?"

"Yes, it does. She keeps saying no, but not with any conviction . . ."

Louise rose majestically. "Then I think it's time you did something."

Iris raised her perfectly spaced eyebrows. "What?"

For answer Louise walked across the room to the small telephone table. Picking up the directory she brought it back to Iris and handed it to her. "I think it's time you made your peace with Rachel."

Iris grimaced and picking up her glass of tomato juice, finished it. "Rachel is as boring as this tomato juice."

"That may be," Louise admitted, "but I'm afraid it's something you'll have to put up with. Unless, of course, you're no longer interested in separating Alice and Eliot."

"Oh, all right." Iris opened the directory, looking for Steve Frame's home telephone number. "It's probably unlisted."

Louise shook her head. "Does that strike you as being like Rachel?"

"No."

"Then keep looking. I'm sure they're in there."

And of course they were.

Iris held out her hand. "Bring me the phone, Louise." Louise reached it over to Iris, then settled down quietly to listen.

"Rachel," Iris said when the connection went through. "It's Iris Carrington." She held the phone a little away from her ear so Louise could hear.

"Oh," Rachel said. "My goodness, Iris. How nice of you to call. How are you?"

"I'm much better, thank you."

"When I heard you were sick with the flu—and such a funny time of year to get it—I mean, funny peculiar—"

"Yes," Iris said, rolling her eyes at Louise. "I understood what you meant, Rachel."

"Well, what I started to say was I was going to send you some flowers. But then—well, what with one thing and another, I never did do it. That's terrible of me, isn't it?" She laughed her nervous little self-depreciating laugh.

Privately Iris agreed that it was, but she only said, "It's perfectly all right, Rachel. I had more flowers than I knew what to do with, Tell me, Rachel, how have you been?"

"Oh, fine. I've been fine, Iris."

"And that big important husband of yours. How is he?"

"Oh, he's fine too."

"And how are—well—things, as you put it, I believe?"

"Between Steve and me, you mean?"

"Yes, Rachel, that's what I meant."

"Oh." The nervous little laugh again. "Things are fine with us, Iris. Wonderful. They couldn't be better."

Once again Iris glanced at Louise. Even over the phone she could hear the strain in Rachel's voice. "In that case, Rachel, there's something I'd like to talk to you about. But not on the telephone. That's such a tiresome mode of communication . . ."

"Yes. It is, isn't it?" Rachel giggled.

Iris sighed to herself, thinking if she said black was white, Rachel would agree with her. "I wonder, could you come have tea with me this afternoon?"

"Why, yes, Iris. That would be nice."

"Wonderful, Rachel. At four o'clock?"

The time agreed on, Iris cradled the phone. Just as she handed it back to Louise there was a knock. "Room service," came through the door.

Louise returned the phone to its little table and opened the door, standing aside as the bellhop pushed the linen-covered cart in, two places set, steam covers over the plates. With elegant efficiency, he removed the covers, poured water into the two glasses, and let himself out.

As they sat down to the table and unfolded the linen napkins in their laps, Louise said, "Do you have a plan for Rachel, Iris?"

"I think so," she answered. "It seems to me that if Steve wants to meet with Alice—and I can't think of any other logical explanation for his phone call to her—then he's more likely to do it if Rachel isn't anywhere around. So my plan is to try to spirit her away." Iris picked up the club sandwich on her plate. "But let's enjoy our lunch, Louise. We're certainly not going to enjoy afternoon tea. At least

I'm not." A sour tone pervaded her voice.

And with that they dropped the subject of Rachel for the time being.

Expecting Rachel to be prompt, Iris had the tea cart delivered at three-forty-five. In fact, she was a few minutes early, apologizing profusely.

"I was counting on more traffic than there was," she said, flouncing and wincing in her nervous little way. Iris having dismissed Louise to the bedroom, answered Rachel's knock herself.

"Sit down, Rachel," she invited, as graciously as she could. "And how lovely you look."

"Do you like it really?" Rachel asked eagerly, glancing proudly at the white batiste dress she was wearing.

"Yes. Very much." Iris herself had dressed very carefully for the occasion, wearing a light-blue sleeveless linen sheath. Louise had fussed over her coiffure, making sure every hair was in place. Smiling grandly at Rachel, Iris said, "Clothes are part of what I wanted to talk to you about. You said once you wished you had my dressmaker."

"Oh! I still do!" Rachel said. "I mean, there's nobody around here who can make clothes like yours."

Iris walked to the tea cart, poured tea for herself and Rachel, and sat down in a chair facing hers.

"Rachel, I'm glad you could come this afternoon. What with Dennis' health—and my own—I've been feeling a bit low, when I got to thinking, 'Wouldn't it be *fun*,'"—here Iris lied wildly—"'to go on a shopping spree with that pretty little Rachel'—just as a sort of wedding present. Rachel, how would you like to meet my dressmaker?"

Rachel's dark eyes went wide. "Is he coming here to Bay City?"

"No. You and I would go to New York and meet him there. And while we're there," she added, sipping her tea, "you could meet my hairdresser as well. You have such lovely hair. I'm sure he could do wonders with it."

Rachel sighed. "Wouldn't that be something?"

Iris smiled. "You make it sound like an impossible dream, Rachel, when it isn't that at all. It's a simple matter of flying to New York, staying a few days at my hotel suite there, making an appointment with the hairdresser and the dressmaker and—" she waved a hand "—*voilà.*"

Putting her cup and saucer down, Iris went back to the tea cart for the plate of watercress sandwiches she had ordered. She put three of the little sandwiches on a smaller plate and passed it to Rachel. "Well," she said, going back to her seat, "what do you say? Does the idea appeal to you?"

"Oh, my goodness, yes," Rachel said. "It certainly does. But whether I can do it or not, I don't know." She picked up a sandwich. "I don't know what Steve would say. I mean, he's so busy, I don't know if he could get away just now."

"I wasn't thinking of Steve going with us, Rachel. I would think such a trip would bore him to death. I was thinking of just the two of us—you and I."

"Oh, my," Rachel said, swallowing her bite of sandwich. "Oh, I don't know, Iris. If he'd want me to go without him, I mean."

"But you said he's so busy."

"He is." Rachel was making a few rapid calculations.

"Well then, surely he wouldn't mind if you went off with me for just a few days. I mean, you did say, Rachel, that things are fine with you and Steve."

Rachel finished the rest of her sandwich. "Oh, yes.

They are. Things couldn't be better."

"Then why don't you ask him when he gets home tonight? I'll have to make plans for our trip, you know. I can't just pick up and go, expecting my hairdresser and my dressmaker to be sitting around waiting for me."

"No, of course, Iris. I understand that."

"Then you'll speak to Steve."

"Yes. Yes, I will."

But she didn't have the chance that night when he got home from work. When Alice didn't return his call, Steve called her again, still without results. When he finally left the office, he was in a very dark mood indeed.

Coming into the living room, setting his briefcase down, he said, "I've tried all day to talk to Alice, but you and that father of yours have seen to it that Alice will never talk to me again—not even to give me a chance to try to explain things to her."

Rachel had been in such a state all day, expecting Steve to blow up at her—and Lord alone knew what else—she hardly knew what she was doing. Iris Carrington's phone call had further unnerved her. Had it been anybody but Iris calling, she wouldn't have accepted the invitation to tea. But Iris was almost as important to her as Steve was, and so she had gone, only to learn that Iris wanted to complicate her life further.

"Steve," she said now, "I didn't have any part in what my father did. I swear to you." She was still wearing the white batiste dress, one that Steve had admired when she first bought it. Today he didn't notice it at all.

"I want the truth, Rachel," he said.

"Steve, that is the truth. I swear it. I didn't know a thing about it until months and months afterward—not until last spring sometime. Not until my father was ready to leave Bay City. That's when he told me what he had done."

Steve was looking at her, his eyes boring into her, "If that's the case, why didn't you tell me about it then?"

She stared at him aghast. "Tell you then? Or any other time? When you're last person in the world I'd want to be told? Steve, I was scared to death you'd find out about it. I was sure I'd lose you if you knew. It's bad enough that you think of Alice all the time anyhow, without—"

He cut her off with a fierce look and in a menacing voice told her, "If I think of Alice all the time, it's because you force me to think about her. Whose idea was it to get married in this house? Whose idea was it to live here? Whose idea was it to honeymoon in the beach house at St. Croix? Whose idea was it to make friends with Iris Carrington—and for what purpose? Why can't you leave Alice alone?"

Badly frightened, as angry at herself as she was at anybody else, she threw caution to the wind. "Why can't Alice leave you and me alone?" she shrilled. "We were perfectly happy until she came back here to Bay City. She didn't have to come back. The Carringtons could have found somebody else to take care of Dennis. No, she wanted to come back, she wanted to come back and make trouble between us. And that's just what she's done, too."

Steve looked like he was ready to tear his hair out—or hers, that the only thing preventing him was the inability to decide whom to start with. "Alice hasn't *done* anything. And if she wants to live here she has a perfect right to. Bay City is her home."

His reasoning only fueled her fire. "You always take her side," Rachel wailed. "You always stand up for her, when she won't even wipe her feet on you. Little Miss Perfect. If she's so perfect, what's she doing having an affair with Eliot Carrington?"

"She's not having an affair with Eliot Carrington. That's a piece of malicious gossip you've been trying to spread all over town. I'll say it again, Rachel—and for the last time. Leave Alice alone."

Unable to get anywhere with Steve by storming at him, Rachel changed her tactics. "I could leave her alone if you would," she said. "Oh, Steve please. Forget Alice. Jamie and I are your family now. We love you. We want you. Please don't walk out on us."

"Then stop giving me reason to."

"Steve, I swear to God I didn't know what my father had done until it was too late, way too late, to undo it. You've got to believe me. You've got to."

"All right," he said, wearied by the strain. "It doesn't make any difference anyhow. The end result was the same." He walked away from her, heading for the stairs.

Still trembling, Rachel ran after him, grabbing his hand. "Steve, I love you. I always have. And we've had some wonderful times together, haven't we?"

"Yes," he admitted. "We have."

"And we can have them again," she said. "Steve, you and I understand each other. We go after what we want. And we get it. Look where you started out and where you've ended up. That's what Alice never appreciated about you. She doesn't know you the way I do."

At the mention of Alice, he tensed again, and when Rachel tried to embrace him, he pushed her away. "Nobody knows me, Rachel, and you least of all." Disgusted, hurt, and confused, Steve picked up his car keys and walked out of the house.

Chapter Eight

Persistence Rewarded

Far from giving up his attempts to explain to Alice how she had been tricked into finding him with Rachel, Steve redoubled his efforts. He continued to call her at Eliot's hotel suite as he had done that first day, but now he also appealed to others to help him reach her.

Beginning with Lenore, at the end of a meeting with his architectural staff, Steve asked her if she would stay behind. When the others had left he closed his office door and turned to her. "Rachel's father was here yesterday. He had quite a story to tell me." And then he went on to relate the episode beginning to end.

She listened, horrified.

When he had finished, he leaned against his desk, arms folded, his dark eyes brooding, intent. "I've got to speak to her, Lenore, but I can't do it if she won't let me."

Lenore, as tender hearted as she was beautiful, frowned up at him. "Have you spoken to anybody else?"

"No, not yet. But I intend to." He pushed away from the desk to pace the room. "Will you speak to her?"

"Of course I will, Steve."

"What worries me," he said, stopping suddenly and turning to face Lenore, "is that Alice knows something about that night that I don't."

"Like what?"

"I don't know what." He resumed his pacing. "If all it amounts to is that she saw me upstairs with Rachel or that she heard what we said to each other, or at least what I said to Rachel, then I won't have any problem. I can explain all that—clear myself if it comes to that. But maybe there's more to it . . ." He shook his head. "Maybe she's read something into that night that I don't know about . . ."

Lenore put out her hand and touched his arm. "Don't make it more complicated than it is. And don't make it harder for yourself, either. I'll speak to Alice. I'll ask her if she knows something you don't."

He squeezed her hand. "Will you, Lenore?"

"Yes. And I'll do it now, I'll call her and make a lunch date with her, or something."

Steve gave her an anxious look. "And will you get back to me as soon as you know anything?"

She patted his arm with her outstretched hand. "The very moment, Steve. The very moment." She stood up. "I'm sure I'll know something before the day is out." With an encouraging smile, she left his office.

But as it turned out, the only thing she knew before the day was out was that Steve was in for more disappointments.

Alice agreed to meet her friend for a sandwich lunch in the park along the bay, in an area near the marina where Dennis would be working out with his physical therapist. Sitting on a bench together, watching the exercises, they ate their sandwiches and drank their sodas, while Lenore got to the business at hand.

"Steve asked me to speak to you, Alice."

Alice nodded, her eyes on Dennis and the therapist. "I suspected as much when you called about lunch." She turned to look at Lenore. "Well, now you've spoken. Next topic."

"Just like that?" Lenore was more than a little surprised.

"Lenore, everything that can be said has already been said."

"Steve thinks you may have misinterpreted something about that night, or that you know something that he doesn't."

Alice busied herself gathering the soda cans and sandwich wrappers. "I don't know what it could be. It seems to me that if anything, it's the other way around. I didn't stay to hear their whole conversation. Just enough to know that Steven had betrayed me." There was a catch in her voice over the last few words.

"But Alice," Lenore pleaded, "there was trickery involved. Do you remember getting the message saying Steve's office had called asking you to stop there to pick him up on your way home?"

Alice gave an impatient shake of her head. "Of course I remember, Lenore."

"But it wasn't Steve's office calling. He knew nothing about that call. Gerald Davis made it, Rachel's father. He wanted you to find them together. He hoped you would do exactly what you did—put two and two together, and whether it came out five or six or seven, run away."

The bright rubber ball that Dennis and his therapist were tossing back and forth to each other came bouncing over to the bench. Lenore retrieved it and threw it back to Dennis, who grinned and shouted, "Thanks, Lenore."

She waved to him. "No sweat, Dennis," she called. Turning back to Alice, she continued. "Won't you at least talk to him, Alice? Let him tell his side of the story?"

"I already know his side of the story."

"You didn't know about Gerald Davis's part in it until I just told you."

"What Gerald Davis did or didn't do is beside the point. The point is I heard Rachel tell Steven she was with him the day I lost my baby, when he had led me to believe he was with one of his field men. Why did he lie to me, Lenore?"

"I don't know, Alice. But surely he can explain that."

Alice nodded. "Yes, I'm sure he can. Probably with another lie."

"Alice, please."

She shook her head. "No, Lenore. I don't want to see him. Or talk to him. I'm sorry. I know how torn you are by all this, but I just can't do it. And tell him to please stop calling me."

Lenore sighed. "All right. I'll tell him, but I doubt he'll pay any attention."

Back in Steve's office Lenore reported on her meeting with Alice. He listened in silence, then went to the window overlooking the street below. "Do you believe that Alice doesn't care about me any longer?"

"No, I don't believe that Steve. I've never believed it."

"Do you think I should stop trying to get her to meet with me?"

For a few moments Lenore didn't answer. Then she said, "Nobody but you can answer that question, Steve."

He drew a few lazy circles in the dust on the window pane, then nodded slowly.

After Lenore had gone back to her own office, he

picked up the phone and called Jim Matthews, Alice's father. Alice's mother had never wholeheartedly approved of him, even when he and Alice were at their happiest, but her father had always been open to him, willing to hear him out.

"I'll speak to her, Steve," he said when Steve had finished. "I don't know if it will accomplish anything, but Alice has always been fairminded, and I'll remind her of that. I'll get back to you after I've talked to her."

But the answer was still no.

The next person Steve turned to was Alice's sister. Pat, like her father, listened to what he had to say, then answered, "I'll do what I can, Steve. I know Alice still cares for you. I don't think she's ever stopped caring. But that's part of the problem."

Steve frowned. "That doesn't make sense, Pat. If she still cares for me, why won't she talk to me?"

"I'm not sure I can explain it to you—not so you'd understand."

"Are you talking about pride?" He could sympathize strongly with that sometimes explosive emotion.

"No. Not pride. Fear!"

"Fear?" he exclaimed, incredulous.

Pat sighed. "Let me talk to her, Steve, and I'll get back to you. Later today if I can."

But the day passed without his hearing from her.

Meanwhile, Steve's calls to Alice at Eliot's hotel suite were being monitored by Iris Carrington, picked up by the electronic bugs and transcribed by the faithful Louise.

Thus encouraged, Iris sent a messenger out to Rachel's house with some designs her dressmaker had sent out, hoping to increase the pressure on Rachel to accompany her to New York. In the note attached to the designs, Iris suggested that some of them would suit Rachel even better than herself. But of course in order to do that, her dressmaker would have to meet Rachel, get her measurements, her skin tones, and other vital information.

"That ought to do the trick," Iris remarked to Louise when the messenger had been dispatched. "She'll go positively ga-ga over some of those designs."

"Yes," Louise agreed. "I'm sure she—"

The telephone rang. Louise answered it, then held the phone. "It's for you. It's Dr. Matthews."

"I was hoping he'd call," Iris said, coming to the phone. "Hello, Russ. How nice to hear from you."

Iris had had dinner or lunch a few times with Russ, had even toyed with the notion of stirring up an affair with the affable young doctor, but nothing much had come of it. Still, they were on friendly terms, and she was more than grateful to him for the miracle he was working with her son.

"I'm calling about Dennis," he said now. "The reports get better and better, Iris."

"That's wonderful! How soon do you think you'll be able to discharge him altogether?"

"I probably shouldn't say, because I don't know yet myself for certain, but I would think well before the end of the year, maybe as soon as a month to six weeks."

"That seems unbelievable, Russ."

"Yes, doesn't it?" he agreed. "Well, I just wanted to give you a verbal preview of our latest report, Iris. I'll put it in the mail to you."

"All right. Thank you."

From what she heard of the conversation, Louise assumed that the news from Russ Matthews had been good. But as Iris set the phone down, she let out a ragged little sigh.

"What is it?" Louise asked, alarmed. "Not bad news?"

"No . . ." Iris sighed again. "On the contrary. Dennis is doing splendidly."

"But . . .?"

"Oh, Louise, there's always bad news with the good, I suppose. Russ may be able to discharge Dennis in as short a time as a month, but once that happens, none of us will have any reason for staying here in Bay City—and certainly not Eliot. He'll go back to New York, and he'll take Alice with him to continue nursing Dennis. And once Alice is away again from Steve—particularly if she's had no reconciliation with him first—then she may give in to Eliot's entreaties."

"Assuming he's making them, Iris."

"You don't think he is." It was more a statement than a question.

The nurse-companion shook her head. "Not with the certainty that you do."

Iris's had come to rely heavily on Louise, especially since her breakdown. But when it came to her relationship with Eliot, she couldn't entirely trust anyone's judgment. Too much was at stake: her future, her self-esteem, and especially her pride. If she had a response to Louise's words, she kept it to herself.

After another fruitless day of trying to reach Alice, Steve came home to find Rachel sitting in the living room immersed in dress designs. "Where did those come from?" he asked, glancing at them.

"From Iris Carrington," she answered. "She wants me to go to New York with her so I can meet her dress designer. And her hairdresser. But I don't know what to tell her."

"If you want to go, go." He busied himself at the bar.

Rachel eyed him, trying to measure his mood. "But what about you?"

"What about me, Rachel? I don't need anybody to look after me."

"Jamie does."

"So, do what you usually do with Jamie when it doesn't suit you to have him around—get your mother to take him."

As if on cue, the kitchen door banged and Jamie appeared in the hall. "Hi, Daddy," the six-year-old said, happily.

"Hi, son." For Jamie's sake Steve put on a bright face and gave his son a bear hug. "What have you been up to?"

"Russian ball."

Russian ball was a one-kid ballgame. One of the disadvantages of living in this house was the lack of neighbor children for Jamie to play with, something neither Steve nor Rachel had given any thought to when Rachel insisted on their living here. As a result he played alone more often than not.

"How about some touch football?" Steve said now.

Jamie's thin face brightened. "Gee, Dad, would you?"

"Sure I will. Just let me get out of these clothes and into a pair of shorts. You go find the football, O.K.?"

"Yeah! Great!"

An hour later they were both worn out and drenched with sweat. Steve bathed Jamie and got him into his pajamas. "You go on downstairs, son, and eat your dinner. I'll be down in a few minutes."

Steve watched Jamie scamper down the stairs, then he

went into the master bedroom to shower and change clothes the second time that day. Emerging from the shower, wrapping a towel around himself, he made a decision he'd been working up to all week. Taking his razor and toothbrush and other toilet articles, he moved them to the guest bedroom and bath down the hall. Then he made the same trip with some of his clothes.

Just then, Rachel came upstairs. "What are you doing?" she asked, her hand clutching the banister.

"What it looks like I'm doing," he said. "Changing rooms."

She followed him into the guest bedroom, watched while he hung his clothes in the closet there. "Is this what you had in mind," she said in a low, bitter voice, "when you made me promise I'd be here for you every night and every morning?"

"I didn't know then what I know now."

"You knew I loved you, Steve. And you still know that." She went over to him, trying to embrace him, but he turned away from her. "Please, Steve," she begged. "Please let me make love to you."

He shook his head. "I'm not interested, Rachel. Now, if you'll excuse me, I want to get dressed." Taking shorts and shirt into the bathroom, he closed the door.

She stood looking at the closed door, her hands working into fists and opening again. Finally she turned and went back downstairs. She was beginning to hate this house she had once so coveted.

The next morning, as the small bus that took Jamie to and from summer day camp pulled out of the driveway, Rachel's mother pulled into it in her ancient blue sedan. Waving to Jamie, she got out of the car and came up the steps. "Hi, Rachel. Can you spare a cup of coffee?"

"Sure, Mom." Rachel held the door for her, and they went into the kitchen.

"What are these?" Ada said, looking at the sketches spread out on the table.

"Some dress designs Iris Carrington sent out to me yesterday by messenger. They're from her dressmaker in New York." Rachel poured out two cups of coffee and brought them to the table, then sat down with her mother. "Aren't they fabulous?"

Ada sifted through them, stopping now and then when one caught her eye. "Not bad. But why did she send them to you?"

Rachel told her, then said, "Steve thinks it's a terrific idea. He practically ordered me to go with her."

Ada set her cup down. "That doesn't sound like Steve to me. I shouldn't think he'd care one way or another."

"Well, he does. He wants me to meet the people who take such great care of Iris. And meet some of her friends too."

Ada poured a little more milk into her coffee. "When are you leaving?" She didn't bother to ask about Jamie, assuming Rachel expected to leave him with her.

"Soon. But I don't really want to go alone. I mean, without Steve."

"So get him to go too."

Rachel shook her dark head. "He won't go. I think he's trying to set up a meeting with Alice."

At that, Ada almost dropped her cup. "Did Steve tell you that?"

"No, his sister Janice did. She said he wants to explain to Alice what really happened the night she left him."

"But you said Alice already knows what happened!"

Rachel felt tears welling up in her eyes. "I know, but it

doesn't do any good telling that to Steve. And anyhow he thinks she might know something about that night he doesn't."

"Such as what?"

"I don't know what. I don't have any idea."

Ada finished her coffee. "It sounds to me like things aren't so great between you and Steve."

"That's not true," Rachel said, forcing her tears back. "Everything's fine with us. It's like I said before. I just don't feel like going alone to New York right now, that's all."

For a few moments Ada watched her in silence, then she said, "Rachel, if Steve wants to see Alice, and Alice is willing to let him see her, then it's going to happen whether you're in New York or not."

For the first time Rachel sipped at her coffee. "I know that, Mom. She's no threat to me. But I'm thinking, too, if I don't go to New York with Iris, that might offend her, and I can't afford that. Iris could be very important to me. Socially, I mean."

Finally, with a shake of her head, Ada said, "Rachel, it seems to me maybe you'd better stay here and protect your marriage. You don't want to go to New York because you're scared to death that while you're there mingling with Iris Carrington's hangers-on, Alice and Steve are going to reconcile. But if that happens, if they do reconcile, then you're not going to need Iris Carrington any longer, so what difference does it make whether or not you offend her?"

Rachel slammed her cup into its saucer. "Because there's not going to be a reconciliation! So far, Alice hasn't even agreed to meet with Steve, and I don't think she will," she finished petulantly. "Anyway, Alice doesn't know how to handle more than one man at a time, and she's all involved with Eliot Carrington now."

Ada rolled her eyes heavenward. "Rachel, you think because you say something, that makes it so."

Rachel gave her mother a sullen look. "I don't care if you believe it or not. It is so." Pushing back from the table she carried her cup to the sink and set it down with a clatter, then spun around to face Ada. "And anyhow, even if Alice does agree to meet with Steve, nothing's going to come of it. So to answer your question, I am going to need Iris Carrinton. I may not need her now, while things are kind of up in the air, but the minute Dennis Carrington is discharged by Russ, he and his father and Alice will be leaving Bay City, and that's when everything will settle back down, and then I'll be running things around here."

Ada had everything and nothing to say to that. Knowing from years of experience with her headstrong daughter, that speaking out would merely be a waste of time and breath, she kept quiet. But she felt in her bones that Rachel's marriage to Steve was as good as over, before it had scarcely even begun.

Later that same morning Iris hired a car and driver to take her out to Rachel's house. As they pulled up in the circular driveway she said to him, "Wait out here. I won't be long. No more than a few minutes."

He touched the visor of his cap. "Yes, ma'am."

"What lovely grounds you have around the house, Rachel," Iris said as she stepped into the front hall.

Rachel beamed. "Yes, aren't they? I just love this house. I love everything about it."

Iris, having followed the local gossip, knew better. Still she smiled politely. "Yes, I'm sure. Well," she continued, following Rachel into the living room, "I've come for your answer, my dear. I made reservations this morning for the two of us to fly to New York tomorrow."

Rachel's heart sank. "That soon."

"I'm afraid so, yes." Iris sat down on the sofa and crossed her long slim legs. "Of course, I can always change the reservation to one. But I hope I won't have to do that. I hate flying somewhere all by myself."

Sitting down across from Iris, Rachel nodded. "Yes. I do too."

Iris gave Rachel a sympathetic look. "And of course I realize my timing isn't the best for you."

"Oh, no, there's nothing wrong with your timing, Iris," Rachel put in hastily. "I mean, everything is fine, really. Steve even said he'd like to go with us, but he can't get away right now. He's such a busy man, you know."

"Oh! Of course!" She arched an eyebrow. "Then I take it your answer is yes, you're going with me."

Feeling somehow she hadn't been given much choice, she answered, "I guess so. Yes."

Iris clapped her hands. "Wonderful, Rachel. I'll have the car here to pick you up at nine o'clock tomorrow morning." She stood up. "And you won't forget to bring the sketches?"

"No. I won't forget them."

Iris fairly glowed. "My dear, you won't regret this. We'll have a wonderful time in New York. And a wonderfully productive time, too. You wait and see."

"I hope so," Rachel said, trying to sound enthusiastic.

Iris squeezed her hand. "I'm sure of it. Well, I must be off. I have a hundred and one things to do."

"Yes," Rachel said. "So do I."

She stood on the front porch watching Iris's car

disappear down the road, then went back into the house to see about her packing, realizing she hadn't asked Iris how long they were going to be gone. She supposed she ought to call her a little later on, when she'd had time to get back to her hotel, then decided with a shrug it didn't matter. Nothing would matter anymore, not if she lost Steve.

Almost before she had finished the thought, she caught hold of herself. She wasn't going to lose Steve, no matter what. She had worked too hard and too long to become Mrs. Steven Frame to let him go, Alice or no Alice. She had beaten Alice before, and could beat her again. No, she thought not could. Would.

While Rachel was packing for her flight to New York, Pat was talking to Alice in the living room of Eliot's hotel suite.

"Darling," she said, "at least give Steve a hearing. You owe him that much."

Alice was stone-faced. "I owe him nothing. Pat, he betrayed me. You know he did."

Pat shook her head. "You say he did, and he says he didn't. You can't both be right."

"And you think I'm the one who's wrong."

Pat looked steadily at her younger sister. "I think you may be. Yes." She put up a hand. "Not deliberately. I don't mean that. But I think you may have misunderstood what you heard. You didn't hear everything they said to each other, did you?"

"No. But I heard enough to . . ." Her voice trailed off.

"Alice," Pat said, "in your own way you've betrayed Steve."

That wasn't what she was expecting to hear. "How do you mean?" she asked, taken aback.

"By running off as you did, not giving him a single word of explanation, not letting him know where you were or how you were or *if* you were. Isn't that a betrayal of trust, if nothing else?"

After a moment Alice spoke, "I suppose so. Yes. But I thought—" She broke off with shrug. "Oh, never mind what I thought. All right, Pat. All right. I'll meet with him."

Pat beamed. "Oh, darling, will you?"

"Yes. But only if you're with me when I do."

"Of course I'll be with you, if you want. Whatever is easiest for you."

"And I don't want to meet on his ground. It has to be on mine."

Seeing her sister so pale and breathless, Pat quickly agreed. "We can do it at Mom and Dad's or at our house or—" She broke off as Eliot Carrington came in.

"I'm sorry to interrupt," he said, looking from her to Alice.

"It's all right," Alice said. "What is it, Eliot?"

"I've just had a call from Los Angeles. I'm going to have to fly out there tonight, but I wanted to check with you first to see if you're free to stay here with Dennis while I'm gone."

"Yes, I'm free, Eliot."

He smiled. "Good. It's the usual thing. Two days. Three at the most."

"Fine," Alice said.

When he had left the room Pat said, "Why don't you meet with Steven here, then—after Eliot goes?"

"I suppose . . ."

"Tomorrow afternoon ?" Pat prompted. "If that's O.K. with Steven?"

"Yes. That's fine with me," Alice replied in a low voice. "May I use your phone?"

"Yes. Of course." Though she felt things were moving a little too quickly.

Pat phoned Steve at his office, saying, "Alice will meet with you, Steve—here, in Eliot's hotel suite. Tomorrow afternoon. How about four-thirty?"

"Whenever and wherever you say, Pat," he answered. "I have to pinch myself to know I'm not making this up."

"You're not, Steve. It's real. I'll talk to you later." She hung up and said to Alice, "It's all set then. He'll come here tomorrow afternoon at four-thirty. And just to make sure nobody get their signals crossed, I'll stop at his office first and come over here with him. How's that?"

Alice hesitated then nodded. "That's fine. I guess."

Pat squeezed her hand. "However it comes out, Alice you won't be sorry."

Tears shimmered on the lashes of Alice's blue eyes. "Won't I, Pat?"

"I don't think so, darling. I really don't."

Pat's conversation with Alice, the interruption by Eliot, the conversation with Steve, the arrangements for the meeting—all were in Louise Goddard's faithfully transcribed notes by the end of the day. Iris read through them with a satisfied smile.

"How I'd love to tell Rachel this," she said. "And what a pity I can't."

Louise shook her head. "It would make a difference in Rachel's plans, all right, but I doubt if it would in Steve's."

"No, I'm sure it wouldn't," Iris said. She put the notes aside. "And now, Louise, I have a favor to ask of you. As soon as Dennis is finished with his lessons tomorrow I

148

want you to take him out to a movie and to dinner afterward, so our two lovebirds can have the hotel suite to themselves for a few hours."

"I can certainly do that. Shall I call Alice now and tell her?"

Iris nodded. "But without telling her why, of course. Make up some reason."

So Louise called Alice, saying Dennis had been working so hard with his lessons, she wanted to give him a little treat tomorrow afternoon. Would it be all right if she took him out to a movie at four o'clock and then to dinner afterward?

"Let me ask him," Alice said.

Coming back to the phone a few moments later she said, "Dennis thinks it's a great idea. And four o'clock is fine."

A smiling Louise reported her success to Iris, and that night, doctor's orders or no, Iris had a small glass of wine. "To celebrate," she said.

But Louise cautioned, "Let's hope you're not being premature."

The next day was a difficult one for Alice to get through. Talking to her mother on the phone in the morning, she said, "I know you don't like the idea of my meeting Steven, Mom."

"Darling," her mother answered, "it's only because I can't stand seeing you hurt more than you already have been."

"You may be expecting something that's not going to happen."

"I wish I could believe that, dear."

Alice clenched the telephone mouthpiece. "Mom, you

and Dad and Russ keep telling me I shouldn't run away from things. Don't you think my meeting with Steven, facing him, listening to what he has to say is the opposite of running?"

"I suppose so."

"Mom," Alice said, feeling a little desperate, "I may find that Steven really doesn't mean anything to me anymore. And if that's so, isn't it better to know I'm free of him than to go on thinking I'm not?"

Hearing the note of desperation in her daughter's voice, she thought she knew Alice's feelings better than Alice herself. But she tried to be encouraging. "You know I'll support whatever decision you make."

As Alice cradled the phone, she reflected that if the hollow feeling in the pit of her stomach meant she no longer cared anything for Steven, it seemed an odd kind of signal.

She sighed with relief when Louise Goddard arrived to take Dennis out, only to find that she was feeling more anxious than ever, a feeling that reached new heights—or depts—when the doorbell rang at four-thirty.

With a swallow—and a glance at herself in the mirror—Alice went to the door to answer it.

Chapter Nine
Grasping at Straws

They were standing in the hall, Steven staring at the carpet, Pat smiling brightly—too brightly. "Well," she said, "we're here. May we come in?"

Alice nodded, her eyes fixed on Pat's face. "Yes. Yes, of course." She opened the door wider, and they passed into the living room of the hotel suite.

"Where's Dennis?" Pat asked. "In his room?"

"No," Alice said, explaining that he was having a night on the town.

"Then why don't I wait in his room?"

Alice panicked. "Pat, you promised!"

"I know what I promised," she said, patting her reassuringly, "and if you insist I'll stay in here with you and Steve. But do you really want me?"

Alice didn't know quite what to say or do. She turned to Steven who, avoiding her glance, stood by a chair. "Steven?" she said. He looked up at her finally, and she found herself turning to mush.

"It's your decision, Alice," he said, his dark, brooding eyes reflecting a riot of emotions seething under the cool demeanor that frightened Alice.

Her decision was a helpless, "I don't know."

"I should think," Pat said, taking matters in hand, "you could both speak more freely without a third person in the room. There might be—there must be things you'd like to say to each other that you'd rather nobody else was listening to. And it isn't as if I'm walking out on you, leaving you really alone. I'll be right in the next room, ready to come out if you call me."

Alice agreed reluctantly. "All right. I guess you're right."

"You'll be fine, darling. And take your time. I brought a book along." With a squeeze of her hand and a smile at Steven, Pat went into Dennis's room and closed the door.

Although it was the first week of fall, it felt more like a middle of August. Alice turned from the sun streaming into the room to say to Steven, "Is it too warm in here for you?"

"No. No, it's fine—unless, is it too warm for you?" he answered solicitously.

"No, No, it's fine. I just thought—well, it doesn't matter. Would you—would you like to sit down?"

"No. I don't mind standing—unless you'd—" He broke off with a shake of his head, his eyes again boring into her. "Oh, Alice, if you knew how long I've waited for this— how many times I've said it all in my head. It seems unreal to me." With his long, raw-boned fingers, he kneaded the back of the armchair his was clutching, as if for dear life. "I think maybe this isn't really happening, anymore than it ever really happened all those other times." He cleared his throat. "Do you know what I mean?"

She knew exactly what he meant, felt the same way he did. "Yes," she breathed. "I know."

He hadn't taken his eyes from her. "And yet you are

real, aren't you? I'm not just making this up."

She shook her head with a small smile. "No, Steven, you're not making it up."

"And you will hear me out? Let me explain what I've wanted to explain to you for all these months—more than a year now?"

This was what she had feared most, why she had fled, had hidden away from him—that he would explain and she would believe, because she was not free of him at all.

"I'm not sure there's anything to explain, Steven. I heard Rachel say you were with her the day I lost the baby. It was Rachel who called on the phone that morning, wasn't it? Not your field man."

He nodded, despair on his face. "Yes. It was Rachel."

"And the other times before that—when the phone would ring and I would answer it, and nobody said anything at the other end, and I thought it was a wrong number—was that Rachel too?"

"I don't know about every time, but one of the times it was. She called one night to say I was going to lose Jamie unless I did something and did it fast, and then she refused to explain what she meant. She wanted me to meet her at Jamie's school the next morning. That was when she told me about Ted wanting to adopt Jamie, and that I could prevent it by letting her come along sometimes when I was with him, that if she was there to discuss various decisions that had to be made about him. I—I would have a better chance—to fight the adoption proceedings."

Steve had been standing a few feet away from her, looking at her. Now he began pacing the room. "I didn't want her along, but I also didn't want to lose Jamie to Ted Clark, so I told her I'd think about it and get back to her. When I didn't do it soon enough to suit her, she called me again—the day you—" he swallowed "—the day we were cleaning out the closet." As Steven said that, he turned to her, the pain in his eyes so intense she could hardly bear to look at him.

"Rachel said she couldn't wait any longer for my decision, something had come up. It turned out it had to do with Jamie's schooling, whether or not he would go to the Holyoke School. She said if I didn't want to have anything more to do with him, just say so, and that would be the end of it. So I agreed to meet her." He turned away, his shoulders sagging as if he had said all there was to say— and knew it wasn't enough.

Alice's brow clouded. "But I don't understand. Why didn't you tell me? Why weren't you honest with me from the beginning?"

His back still to her, his voice muffled, he said, "Because the first time I didn't have time to think. Because it wasn't the first time. There had already been a time before that when I—Alice, do you remember when Rachel asked you to ask me to let Jamie go on thinking that Ted Clark was his father?"

Alice nodded. "Yes, I remember."

"All right. Some time after that—a couple of days, maybe, I don't remember—she turned up in my office saying she knew Ada was the only one who was supposed to have any contact with me about Jamie, but Ada was out of town, and this was so important it couldn't wait for Ada to get back from wherever she'd gone." Steven started pacing again. "I asked Rachel what it was, and she said she wanted to thank me for agreeing to let Jamie go on thinking Ted was his father." Steven stopped at the French windows that opened onto a small balcony overlooking the bay.

Alice waited for him to go on with his story. "And?" she prompted.

He turned from the window to her. "And nothing. That was it."

"But what was so important it couldn't wait for Ada to get back?" She was genuinely puzzled.

"What you've just heard. Her thanking me."

"But that doesn't make sense."

"Exactly. Alice, when I came home that night I intended to tell you about Rachel's visit, but while I was going over it in my head, I asked myself how in the world could I make you believe that was all there was to it?"

Alice felt light-headed. "But Steven," she said, "there had to be more to it than that."

He bowed his head. "You see? Even now you don't believe me." He turned back to the French windows. They were open, and a light breeze floated in off the bay. "Oh, granted there may have been more to it as far as Rachel was concerned. I thought of that then, too—that maybe the whole thing was a deliberate ploy on her part to get me to tell you something she knew in advance you'd never buy." With a shake of his head, he turned back to her. "I don't know. But I did know I couldn't risk telling you. You were so touchy about Rachel, so jealous. I couldn't talk to you about it. But Alice, I swear to you, the only times I ever met with him, the only substance of any of those meetings was Jamie." He looked at her with hope and then with hope fading. "You don't believe me, do you?"

"It isn't that. Or not exactly anyhow." She felt pulled in two directions. "I keep thinking of what I heard Rachel say to you that night, in the apartment."

"What was it? Tell me. Alice, tell me, please."

She closed her eyes, not so much to shut him out as to

relive the painful moment. "I can hear her saying it. I've gone over it and over it so many times in my head."

"Alice, tell me. Please."

She opened her eyes. "She asked you why you were so frightened of seeing her. She said you set up the agreement about seeing Jamie without having any contact with her not for my sake but your own, and why couldn't you admit it? She said you and she had more in common than anybody knew."

Alice's eyes filled with tears. Wiping at them with the back of her hand, she said, "And then she said—and this I can quote to you exactly—she said, 'That day when Alice lost her baby and we were together, I felt closer to you than I've ever felt to another man.'"

"Alice," Steven said, his longing for her plain on his face, "that isn't so. If you thought Rachel and I—" He shook his head vigorously. "That was just Rachel talking, trying to convince me I felt about her the way she felt about me—or said she did."

She was crying now. "Steven, don't. You married her, didn't you?"

He answered her in a voice so low she had to strain to hear him. "When I thought you were lost to me, yes. To give my son a name."

"And only for that reason?"

He looked at her a moment. "Alice," he murmured, "I'm an ordinary man with ordinary feelings. I can also be bitter and self-pitying. I couldn't understand how you could walk out on me without a word of explanation, without giving me a chance to hear what I'd done, when so far as I knew I hadn't done anything. I didn't know you were there when I met with Rachel that night. The whole thing had been arranged at the last minute. I didn't want to bother you about it at the hospital, I never liked calling you there unless it was urgent, because I never knew what I might be taking you away from. But I was going to tell you I had met with Rachel the minute I got home. Only when I got home you were gone."

He stood staring out the windows in silence. Beyond the French windows and the balcony, a few sailboats were out in the bay, their white sails set against the brilliant blue sky. "You couldn't have heard all of what transpired that night between Rachel and me. You couldn't have."

"No," Alice said, shaking her head and wiping at the tears with a handkerchief. "When I heard what I just told you—what she said—I turned and ran out."

There were tears in his eyes now too. "And kept on running."

"Yes."

He held a hand out to her. "Alice, if you had stayed, you would have heard me straighten Rachel out on a few things, including that I wasn't interested in her, that whatever had happened between her and me had happened a long time ago. And that it never would have happened at all if I hadn't been lonely and miserable and vulnerable at the time."

Alice continued his thought in a choked voice, "The same way you were feeling when you married her?"

He nodded. "Yes. That's right. Alice, the only injustice I've ever done you—wittingly—was after your father came to the house and took your things away, when I said I no longer cared about you or was interested in you. That wasn't true then. It isn't true now."

She sat down and buried her face in her hands.

"Alice, I love you. I love you more than I've ever loved anybody or anything. I never stopped loving you."

"Oh, Steven," she murmured helplessly.

"And I'd give anything to have you back."

She shook her head. "It isn't possible."

He moved toward her. "Alice, anything is possible it only you'll say you still love me. You love me and you want me."

When she looked up, he was standing near enough to touch her, his dark, brooding gaze resting on her. "Alice, do you love me?"

She couldn't speak.

"Do you?"

She nodded, and reaching down, he took her in his arms.

"Oh, Steven," she said, clinging to him, "yes, I love you. I tried to forget you—to forget you ever existed. But I couldn't. I can't."

"Darling," he said, pulling her to him and kissing her hair lightly. "My darling, my own."

He would have kissed her again, but she twisted away from him. "No. No, it's too late for us now. Steven, please." She backed away from him. "Don't touch me. It only makes things worse. It was hard enough before." She was trembling violently.

"Alice, it's not too late. I'll get free of Rachel."

"How?"

"You let me worry about that. It may take a while—it probably will take a while—but I'll do it." His eyes were ferocious now. "Only, Alice, you have to promise me you won't leave me again."

The tears began anew, swelling from the liquid blue of her eyes, streaming down her cheeks. "I promise, Steven."

He reached out to take one of her hands in his. "And you'll wait for me—however long it takes?"

"Yes, Steven. I'll wait," Alice vowed.

He moved as if to take her in his arms again, but she shook her head. "No, Steven, we mustn't. As hard as this is, that makes it even harder."

He backed off. "I guess you're right."

"And we'd better not see each other either. Not until you can work something out."

"All right," he said, but he eyed her anxiously. "You won't change your mind, will you? You won't decide after I leave here that it's too complicated or it will take too long or you're not really sure you love me that much?"

"No, Steven." She smiled, a small smile at first that grew bigger and bigger until it became the familiar radiant smile of their happy times together. "I love you, my dearest. I'll wait for you. If it takes forever."

Steve was in such a jubilant state after leaving Alice he hardly knew what to do with himself. For a time he drove aimlessly about Bay City, then on impulse he went to see Lenore. While he was with her, his sister Janice called to say Rachel had called him at the office from New York and wanted him to call her back.

Lenore offered the use of her phone, but Steve declined. "I'm not going to call her from here or anywhere else," he said, coming back to sit beside Lenore on the sofa. "I'm in no mood to talk to Rachel tonight."

"I can understand that," Lenore said, "but I think you'd better tell her you saw Alice as soon as she gets back. Word is bound to get around about it, and you don't want her hearing it from somebody else."

He shook his head. "No, I suppose you're right."

She had poured each of them a glass of chablis. Now, sipping it, she said, "It isn't going to be easy, you know, freeing yourself of Rachel. She worked long and hard to become Mrs. Steven Frame, and she isn't going to want to give that up."

"She can go on being Mrs. Steven Frame for all I care, as long as I don't have to be a part of it. And I don't think I will be if I offer her enough money. That's the main reason she married me in the first place."

Lenore didn't agree with him. "Not entirely. That and to prove to Alice she could bring it off."

"Yeah, I suppose you're right." He sighed. "Lord, what a fool I've been, and I don't ever seem to learn."

The truth in that remark was emphasized the next afternoon when Steve stopped by John Randolph's law offices to tell him he wanted to get a divorce from Rachel.

A lawyer sees and hears a lot of human nature, but John mastered his shock at this revelation only with great difficulty. "A divorce? On what grounds?"

Steve had a ready answer. "Fraud. Gerald Davis called the hospital and tricked Alice into finding me that night with Rachel, and Rachel was in on it."

John scratched his chin, musing. "As I understand it, Rachel maintains she didn't know what her father had done until several months later."

"Rachel maintains," Steve said sourly. "John, how many lies has Rachel told in the last few years that you know about?"

"Too many to count, I know. But charging fraud and proving it—especially when you're talking about proving it in a courtroom—are two different things. As things stand now, it's your word against hers, with no corroboration on either side." John straightened the edges of a pile of papers on his desk. Then he looked at Steve. "Have you said anything to Rachel?"

"No. Not yet. She called me a little while ago to say she was coming back from New York tonight. I tried to get her to stay on for a few more days, but she wouldn't."

John frowned. "To what end?"

"I don't know. Because I don't have anything to say to her, I guess."

"On the contrary, Steve," John exclaimed. "You have a great deal to say to her. What's more, I think you ought to give some thought to exactly what you're going to say, and how best to proceed."

Steve, however, was a man of action. "What other way is there to proceed except to tell Rachel straight out I want a divorce? If I don't have any grounds to file for one, then I'll give her grounds. I'll desert her."

"And what if she doesn't choose to file? What then?"

Steve didn't like what he was hearing. It hadn't occurred to him that there was going to be any real problem in separating himself from Rachel. "There must be ways of persuading her," he said. "No divorce, no money. Something like that."

John gave him a doubtful look. "Money is a factor, of course. But I think you also have to take her feelings into consideration."

He snorted, saying harshly, "Don't bring love into this. Rachel doesn't love me. John. The only person Rachel has ever loved is Rachel."

"That may be. But she went to considerable effort to get you to marry her."

"Because she loves being my wife."

"Exactly. You've pinpointed the problem. Rachel loves being your wife. She's not going to give that up without a fight."

Steve had indeed pinpointed the problem: Not only did

Rachel love the idea of being Steve's wife, she was not about to hand him over to Alice. It galled her further that she had to hear all about this latest development from Iris Carrington.

Louise Goddard had transcribed the meeting between Alice and Steve and, on her return from New York, gave the papers to Iris who read them with ill-concealed delight. Without hesitation, she called Rachel to say she had something of interest for her. Rachel arrived in the hotel suite in due course, and Iris had no more than exchanged greetings with her, when she hurried her to a seat and played the tape for her.

Rachel listened, horrified and incredulous. Which were the sentiments she expressed when the tape ended.

Two days of constant companionship with Rachel in New York had been almost more than Iris could bear. Turning impatiently to her now, she said, "Surely you don't think I hired two people with voices like Steve's and Alice's—and wrote a script as well for them to read?"

Rachel reddened. "I didn't mean that."

"Then what exactly did you mean?"

In her distress Rachel forgot for a moment whom she was talking to. "It's just that I can't believe—well, I suppose I knew Steve would get somebody to talk Alice into seeing him, but I never thought—I mean, I thought she was so involved with—" Her hand flew to her mouth. "Oh!" she gasped. "Never mind."

Iris knew very well what Rachel was referring to, but since she herself, working through Louise, had planted that story about Alice and Eliot with Rachel, she could hardly criticize her now. Ignoring the insinuation, she said, "I can see now why Steve wanted you in New York."

Rachel was still red in the face, but she was moving

quickly from anguish to anger. "It won't do him any good," she snapped. "I have no intention of giving him up, to Alice or anybody else. He can't divorce me—I haven't given him any reason to. And there's no reason he could give me, none, that would persuade me to divorce him. So that is that."

Driving to her mother's house from the hotel, she was still so angry and upset that she came close to colliding with the car in front of her when the light at the approaching intersection turned red. Slamming on the brakes, she missed the car by a hair's-breadth, then cursed the other driver for making her stop so short.

"Well," her mother said when she opened the front door to her, "I didn't know you were back."

"I just got back," Rachel said. "I came to pick up Jamie." She sailed past Ada into the house.

Her mother followed her inside. "He isn't home from school yet."

"Then I'll wait for him." Rachel sat down on the living room sofa.

Her mother stood in the doorway eyeing her with trepidation. "Something's happened. What is it? Didn't you have a good time in New York?"

"It has nothing to do with New York. Or maybe it does. Anyhow—" And she told her mother about the meeting between Alice and Steve and how it had all been taped. Then she said, "They can fall in each other's arms if they want to. For all I know, they already have. But I'm Mrs. Steven Frame now, and I intend to go on being Mrs. Steven Frame. I'm never going to give him up. Never."

Ada walked into the living room and sat down in a chair near the sofa. *So I was right about Rachel's marriage*, she said to herself, though the thought gave her little satisfaction. Aloud, she said, "How can you go on living with a man who doesn't love you, Rachel?"

Rachel glared at her. "How can you go on taking their side against me?" She shook her dark head. "My own mother."

Ada sighed. "Honey, I'm only trying to get you to look at things the way they are instead of the way you want them to be."

Rachel made a face. "The way things are is I'm Mrs. Steven Frame. And that's also the way I want them to be. So for once, Mom, you're wrong."

"Rachel, I'm not talking about a name on a piece of paper. I'm talking about feelings."

Rachel could hardly contain herself. "And don't you think I have any feelings? I love Steve. I've loved him ever since I first set eyes on him. It took me a long time to get him away from Alice, but I got him—and I aim to keep him."

Ada gave a little cluck. "I've known for a long time, Rachel, that you don't listen to me, but I think now you don't even listen to yourself. Did you hear what you just said?"

Rachel frowned. "What's that?"

"'It took me a long time to get him away from Alice.' Those were your exact words, Rachel."

"Well? So?"

Ada shook her head. "What have you just been complaining to me about? That Alice was trying to get Steve away from you. It seems to me she's only trying to get back what you took in the first place."

"It's not the same."

"What's different?"

"For one thing, Jamie. I'm his mother. Steve's his father.

Steve had no right to marry Alice when he already had a son."

Ada wanted to point out that Rachel had had no right conceiving Jamie with Steve Frame when she was already married to Russ Matthews, but she held her tongue. She was alarmed at what Rachel might be planning to do regarding Jamie. "Rachel," she said, "for all the wrongheaded things you've done these last few years, you've always been a good mother to Jamie. A good mother and a loving one. Don't spoil that now by using Jamie to try to keep Steve."

Rachel gave her a sulky look. "I don't know what you mean."

"Yes, you do. However this all works out, Rachel, you're going to get hurt. You're already hurting. Well, don't make Jamie suffer too. Don't turn him into some kind of volleyball to be batted back and forth."

Rachel gave her a hard look and said, "You let me worry about Jamie. I'm the one who's been doing it ever since he was born, since *before* he was born. I'm not going to stop doing it now, and I'm not going to do anything to hurt him, either. It's Steve and Alice who want to do something that will hurt him. *That's* what I'm trying to stop." Her eyes were like chips of glass now. "That's what I'm *going* to stop."

After leaving her mother's house Rachel drove home, a bit calmer now that she had been able to vent some of her rage. She decided she would stop talking to people who were against her and talk instead to one person who wasn't. Maybe she could get some help there.

That one person was Steve's sister, Janice, who still lived at the house with them. As soon as Janice arrived from the office, Rachel dragged her into the living room and showed her the tape Iris had given her, explaining what it was and where it had come from.

Janice asked flatly. "What do you expect me to do about it, Rachel?"

Taken aback by Janice's cool reception of this latest outrage, Rachel flushed. "Well, I need your help."

Janice was not moved. "I don't know what help I can give you. Steve doesn't wait around for me to tell him what to do, he does things on his own."

Rachel frowned. "But he'll listen to you, Janice."

"Sometimes he does. Sometimes he doesn't."

Rachel couldn't believe this. Janice had been a firm ally of hers almost from the moment of their meeting some months earlier. "I don't understand," she said. "I mean—well, you can't want Steve to go back to Alice, not after the way you feel about her."

"How I feel about her isn't how Steve feels about her. Look, Rachel, I've already talked to Steve about you and about Alice. He told me how you lied to him, how you lie to everybody—and how you use people to get what you want."

Rachel stared at her. "That's not true!"

"Well, true or not, I'm opting out of this."

"Y-you mean," Rachel stuttered, "you won't help me try to keep Steve?"

"That's right."

"But I thought you were my friend."

Janice sighed. "Rachel, I'm Steve's sister. If it comes to choosing sides between you, would you expect me to go against my own brother?"

"If it's for his own good, yes."

"And who's to decide that, Rachel? You? I've heard people say you're not very bright, and I'm beginning to see why. Now, if you'll excuse me, I want to get freshened up before dinner."

Janice went upstairs, thinking she had better make plans to find a place of her own. Unless Rachel moved out, and that seemed very unlikely, this house would soon be an impossible place to live.

For her part, Rachel stood in the living room watching Janice go upstairs and thinking she would now have to take her tape where she should have taken it to begin with, where it would do the most good. To Alice.

Chapter Ten
Renewed Vows

When the doorbell rang at the Matthews' house, Mary thought it was the postman with a package she was expecting. When she opened the door she was astonished, and not at all pleased, to see Rachel standing there.

Through all the years of her marriage to Russ Matthews Rachel had never felt comfortable with her mother-in-law. She had been in awe and afraid of her, always conscious of her deficiencies in manners and education. Now, however, she was too angry and upset by the threat Alice posed to her marriage to Steve Frame to care what Mary Matthews might be thinking about anything. "Hello, Mrs. Matthews," she said, sharply.

Mary's response was even more abrupt. "What do you want?" was all she said.

"I want to see Alice. May I come in?"

"No, you may not."

Mary would have closed the door on her, but Rachel put her foot on the threshold so she couldn't. "I think you'd better hear what I have to say."

With the door only ajar, Mary said, "Very well, then.

Say it." She gave Rachel a withering look.

Up went Rachel's chin in the familiar gesture of defiance. "How would you like to see Alice made the laughingstock of Bay City?" When Mary didn't answer, she continued, "Because that's what I'm going to do to her if you don't let me into this house to see her."

"Rachel—" Mary began, but she got no further. At that moment Alice came into the living room from the kitchen, and hearing Rachel's name, joined her at the front door. "Mom, what is this? Rachel, what are you doing here?"

Mary tried to get between them. "Don't talk to her, Alice. Don't have anything to do with her. She's making threats."

"That's right," Rachel said, with no effort to keep her voice down. "I intend to carry them out, too, Alice, if you don't talk to me."

Alice turned to her mother. "Let her in, Mom. You might as well, if you don't want the whole neighborhood to hear her."

Mary grudgingly opened the door wider and in she came. "I don't like this," Mary said.

Once inside Rachel turned to her former mother-in-law. "I want to talk to Alice alone."

"You'll talk to her under conditions we set up," Mary said stiffly, "or you won't talk to her at all."

"It's all right, Mom," Alice said. "I can handle this." She supposed Rachel had found out somehow about her meeting with Steven in Eliot's hotel suite, maybe Steven had talked with her already and she was here to make some other demand—like get lost, and stay there.

Alice's mother looked from her to Rachel and back again. "I'll be in the kitchen if you need me, dear."

She had no sooner left the living room than Rachel said, "This isn't private enough."

"Then we'll go into Dad's study and shut the door. Will that suit you?"

Rachel nodded. "Yes."

Inside the study, the door closed, Alice said, "All right, Rachel. What do you want?"

"I want you to listen to something I've got here." She reached into her tote and took out a small tape recorder. Snapping the reels into place, she set the "Play" button.

Alice listened in silence as she heard Pat say, "There might be—there must be things you'd like to say to each other that you'd rather nobody else was listening to." And then came all the things she and Steven had said to one another thinking they were alone. When the tape was finished, Alice turned to Rachel. "Where did you get this?"

Rachel's face twisted into an ugly sneer. "What difference does that make? The point is I have it, the same as I have Steve, Alice. I have him, and I'm not going to let him go."

Alice's head was high, her backbone straight and firm. "You've never had him, Rachel, any way but physically. He doesn't love you, and what's more, he never has."

Rachel flushed. "That's not true."

Alice shook her head. "Instead of busying yourself playing the tape, Rachel, try listening to it. Didn't you hear him say in his own words why he married you? For the same reason Jamie was conceived: because he was lonely and miserable and vulnerable at the time. Because he thought I was lost to him for good."

Rachel sneered at her. "You? He's never loved you."

To prove her point Alice rewound the tape until she

located the spot she was looking for. Then she pressed the "Play" button. "Alice, I love you," Steve was saying. "I love you more than I've ever loved anybody or anything. I never stopped loving you."

"Oh, Steven," she heard herself say.

"And I'd give anything to have you back."

"It isn't possible."

"Alice, anything is possible if only you'll say you love me still. You love me and you want me."

Rachel stopped the tape, then put the recorder back in her tote. "Words, words, words," she said in the same sneer, "and you're naive enough to believe them. Steve doesn't love you, and he never has. He loves what you stand for. The beautiful, blond, blue-eyed virgin. The girl from the right side of the tracks, from a family whose name means something, the girl with the proper upbringing, the girl he can put on a pedestal and worship, the girl he will always reach for and never be able to have. Yes, have, Alice. Physically, and in every other way."

"That's a lie," Alice said.

"Is it? I'm not the only one who lies, Alice, but at least when I do it I know what I'm doing. Sure, Steve *thinks* he loves you. Sure, he *thinks* you're the only girl in the world who matters to him, but that's not so. When you walked out on him that last time, if he wanted you back why didn't he come after you?"

"He didn't know where I was."

Rachel scoffed, "And he didn't have enough money to try to find out? Don't make me laugh. But O.K., if that's the way you want to play it, let's go on to something else. When the hearing on your divorce was coming up, you were right here in Bay City. Right here in this house. He knew where you were then, all right. If he wanted you back so much, why didn't he come beat down the door to talk to you?"

Alice shook her head. There was no point in talking about Steven to Rachel. But she made one more try. "Rachel, there are a lot of things you don't understand, that you'll never understand."

But Rachel was listening only to her own logic—and her own desires. "There are a lot of things I do understand," she needled, "including Steve—something you never did and never could. Steve and I are alike, Alice, whether you're willing to admit it or not. We're the same kind of people. And I'll tell you something else. You said Steve has never loved me. I think I'm in a better position to judge that than you are."

Alice pointed to the tote, where Rachel had put the recorder and its tapes. "I was only telling you what Steven said to me, Rachel. Do you think you're a better judge of his feelings than he is?"

Rachel's reply was vehement. "Yes, I do! When Steve asked me to marry him, he loved me. And do you know why? Because you weren't here to get in the way, to give him all those grand illusions he has about you and him—those storybook dreams. Because he'd forgotten you—the same as he'll forget you this time when you leave."

"You can stop right there, Rachel," Alice said, putting her hand up. "I'm not leaving this time. I'm staying."

"What for? To wait for Steve to be free of me? Forget it, Alice. It's not going to happen."

Alice went to the door of the den and opened it. "You can't threaten me, Rachel."

"Oh, yes, I can." She took the recorder out of the tote. "What do you think a judge would think about this?"

Still standing by the open doorway, Alice shrugged.

"What it is, Rachel. Try blackmail."

"All right," Rachel said, flushing. "Then let's leave the judge out of it. How would you like to see this copied for a newspaper to splash all over its front page?"

Alice looked at her. "And for Jamie to read along with everybody else in town?"

That took the wind out of her sails. "I was keeping Jamie out of this."

"If you were," Alice retorted, "it was only to save him for some better use."

"Yes," Rachel said, suddenly sly again, "that's right." A different tone crept into her voice now, one that made Alice go cold with fear. "And I'll tell you what it is. Then we'll see if you're still so determined to stay here in Bay City. If Steve divorces me to marry you, he'll never see Jamie again. Never. I can promise you that."

"You don't know what you're talking about," Alice said. "Steven has some say about Jamie."

Rachel snorted. "Steven, as you so sweetly call him, has no say. Of course, maybe Steven doesn't care. Maybe he'll decide his son—his only son—doesn't mean that much to him. Maybe he's willing to give up everything for you, including Jamie."

Though he may have been willing, Alice doubted it. And she had long ago decided she would never come between Steven and his son, would never force him to make that choice. Rachel had found the wedge she was seeking.

"It's your decision, Alice," she was saying. "And now I guess we don't have anything more to say to each other, do we? It's been nice, Alice. It's been real nice." She smiled a nasty smile. "Sort of like old times being her." She swept past Alice out of the den, and out of the house.

Alice was still standing in the den when her mother came in a few minutes later. "Alice," she said, "what is it? What did Rachel say to you?"

Alice didn't answer, but when Mary put a hand on her daughter's arm, Alice crumpled against her. "Oh, Mom, I've lost him," she cried. "I've lost him for good now. It doesn't matter that we love each other. It isn't any use."

"Darling," Mary said, leading Alice to the love seat in the corner, "what is it? What could she possibly have against you?"

Alice shook her head. "It isn't what she said about me. It's what she threatened to do. She said if Steven divorces her, she'd see to it he never sees Jamie again. I can't take Steven away from Jamie. It would break his heart."

Mary comforted Alice as best she could, but she was almost as distressed as her daughter at this new development, for it only meant that, if Alice continued to keep Steven Frame in her life and emotions, that she was in for more heartbreak and unhappiness.

When Jim came home from work that night, Mary told him what had happened, saying she hoped Alice realized now that there was no future for her and Steve.

Settling himself in his favorite armchair with the evening paper, Jim said, "I doubt she'll be swayed that easily."

"That easily?" Mary stared at him. "If you had heard Alice sobbing after Rachel left here you wouldn't use that word."

He unfolded the paper to the sports section. "Just because Rachel makes threats doesn't mean she'll be able to carry them out. She's made threats before."

"Yes," Mary said, "and she's carried them out, too. I don't like what's happening. I don't like it at all."

Before Jim could reply, the doorbell rang. It was Steve asking for Alice. She had gone back to Eliot's hotel suite to stay with Dennis in his father's absence, but Mary wouldn't have told Steve that. She wouldn't have told him anything at all if Jim hadn't called to her from the living room. "Mary," he said, "Alice and Steve are two grown-up people. If they want to communicate with one another, they have a right to do so."

"Oh, all right," Mary said, still keeping Steve in the doorway. Telling him where Alice was, she added, "But I want you to know, Steve, by calling there or trying to see her, you'll only make her more miserable than she already is."

Aware that Mary still disapproved of him, but not understanding this outright hostility, he frowned. "I don't understand," he said. "Has something happened I don't know about?"

Mary nodded. "Rachel was here today."

"Rachel? What did she want?"

Mary gave him a bitter look. "What does Rachel ever want except to make trouble?" She told him about Rachel's threat regarding Jamie, then went on to say, "Jamie is the best weapon Rachel has ever had where you and Alice are concerned. She hasn't hesitated to use him before, and she won't hesitate now. The fact that she came here today to do just that ought to convince you."

Steve tried to reassure her. "You don't understand, Mary," he said. "Rachel doesn't have the sole say where Jamie is concerned."

"Doesn't she?" Mary snapped. "You've never had any legal rights to Jamie."

"I do now."

"That has yet to be proved." With that, Steve pushed

into the house and strode into the living room, with Mary close behind. "And anyhow," she went on to say, "we've gotten away from what concerns me most, and that's Alice's happiness."

Steve cocked an eyebrow. "That's what concerns me most too."

"If that were true, Steve," Mary said, "then you'd get out of Alice's life and stay out of it."

He knew Mary barely tolerated his presence there, but he looked her straight in the face and said, "If Alice wanted me to get out of her life I would. But she doesn't."

Mary's retort to that was, "Alice doesn't know what she wants."

Jim had folded his paper but had otherwise kept out of the exchange between Mary and Steve. Now, however, he spoke up. "Mary," he said, "I know you're concerned about Alice's happiness. I am too. But neither of us can live her life for her. She has to make her own decisions."

Mary was not about to back down. "There are some decisions," she said, "that have been taken out of her hands. Steve is married to Rachel now."

"I'm not going to stay married to her," Steve cut in. "John is going to start divorce proceedings."

Mary turned on him. "On what grounds? You can't decide you want a divorce and get one, just like that."

Steve shrugged. "I know it's not going to be easy, Mary, but it's going to happen. I guarantee it."

"You can guarantee nothing," she replied, "except that you'll hurt Alice a great deal in the process." Mary shook her head. "Can't you understand, Steve, that when you married Rachel, Alice was lost to you forever?"

"I don't believe that, and neither does Alice. And one of these days maybe you won't either. Look, I don't like to disturb Alice when she's with Dennis. Will you ask her to call me?"

Mary very likely would have said no, but Jim spoke up again. "I'll tell her, Steve."

After Steve had gone Jim said to Mary, "Darling, if Alice does go back to Steve, you're going to have to accept it whether you like it or not."

"We'll cross that bridge when we come to it," Mary said stiffly, "and that may be never." With that, she walked out of the living room into the kitchen, and Jim reopened his newspaper with a sigh and a shake of his head.

When Alice reported to Eliot Carrington that her reconciliation with Steven had been tape-recorded he was first disbelieving, then angry. Without bothering to call ahead, he went to Iris's suite and knocked on the door. Louise Goddard opened the door to him, backing off a bit when she saw the look on his face.

"Is Iris here?" he asked.

"Yes. In the living room." Louise ushered him in, then excused herself. Closing herself in her room, she stood ear to the door to hear what was being said between the two Carringtons, though it seemed to be Eliot who was doing the talking.

"How long has my suite been bugged, Iris?" he demanded, refusing the chair she had offered him.

She tried to look like the injured party. "What makes you think I know anything about your suite being bugged, Eliot?"

He would have none of it. "Iris, don't waste my time. I don't have that many enemies."

"I'm not your enemy, Eliot."

"Then why do you treat me like one?" He started pacing

back and forth in front of her. "What were you trying to pick up—proof of infidelity? If so, you've wasted a lot of money. And you've done something more than that, Iris. You've given *me* some proof. I never would have believed you would stoop so low as to employ a professional snoop. Well, I know better now. You're beneath contempt, Iris. Beneath contempt." And he left, letting the door slam behind him.

Louise stayed where she was until Iris had had a chance to absorb Eliot's attack and put on whatever face she could. But one thing was certain: If Iris had harbored a hope that she and Eliot could be reconciled, that hope was now blasted.

As soon as they could arrange it, Steve and Alice met at Lenore's house. Closeting himself there with her while Lenore busied herself elsewhere, Steve reported that Rachel had been as adamant with Steve as she had been with Alice: She was not going to divorce him or give him any grounds for divorcing her.

"It's all right, darling," Alice said. "We both knew it wasn't going to be easy." They were sitting together on the sofa, but keeping a safe distance between them.

"I'm sorry about her coming there and getting you all upset."

Alice smiled. "That's all right too—now that I've had some time to think about it. We couldn't very well expect her to make it pleasant for us. She wouldn't be Rachel if she did."

"No," he said, "I suppose you're right."

He wanted to take her in his arms and hold her close, protect her from Rachel, from anything or anybody threatening her. Now, seated beside her, wanting her so much he ached, he merely reached out and touched his finger to her cheek. "Is everything still O.K.?"

She kissed the finger and put his hand back on his knee. "If by everything you mean you and me, then yes, everything is more than O.K. It's fine."

In his frustration he stood up and walked to the mantel. "It all goes so slowly—when it goes at all."

She followed him lovingly with her limpid blue eyes. "Steven, one of the things on our side is time. We have our whole lives ahead of us."

"I know. I try to think that way myself, but it doesn't help." He sighed, and toyed with a small statue of a Dresden shepherdess. "Sometimes it seems to me I'll be tied to Rachel forever."

"Lenore told me you've been traveling a lot."

He nodded. "As much as I possible can. It's one way to ease the strain." He told Alice how he had moved into the guest bedroom. "What I'd like to do," he continued, "is move out altogether, go back to the apartment above the office. But if I do that, John thinks it's a tantamount to handing Jamie over to Rachel, and I'm not going to do that."

"Darling, I wouldn't want you to."

Carefully he set the statue back on the mantel and stood looking at her, clenching and unclenching his fists. *This*, he thought to himself, *will be the hardest part of all.* John Randolph had also warned him against seeing or embracing Alice, if he didn't want to give Rachel grounds for an alienation of affections suit.

Alice frowned. "What is it, Steven?"

He stilled his hands and tried to give her a reassuring smile. "Nothing." He cast about in his mind for something to talk about that was unrelated to his campaign against

Rachel. "I ran into Russ the other day downtown at lunch. He said you're going back to the hospital, back to your old job."

Alice nodded. "Yes. As soon as Dennis doesn't need me anymore, and that will be any day now."

"Who decides that?"

"Oh, Russ. And Eliot, I guess."

He tried to speak carelessly. "What does Eliot have to say?" Nothing, it seemed, was unrelated to his campaign against Rachel—to the reason for it.

Alice didn't answer immediately. Steve came back to sit, not beside her—that was too much of a temptation—but in an armchair near the sofa.

"You don't mean about Dennis do you?"

He shook his head. "No. About you."

"He's been very understanding, Steven."

He was almost afraid to ask his next question. "Alice, you don't . . ." His voice trailed off.

"No," she said, shaking her head. "Nothing happened between us, Steven. Not now, and not before. But he is a good man. I like him a great deal."

This he had to say, had to get out in the open. "He loves you."

Alice didn't agree to that. "I don't know. I really don't. He may have, but I explained everything to him. I don't think any of it surprised him, Steven. I think he's known all along, right from the beginning and in spite of what I might have said, that I couldn't forget you, that I still loved you."

Steve had always thought well of Eliot Carrington. Now he began to like him. "Might he go back to Iris?"

"No. That's finished. It was finished a long time ago, only Iris wouldn't accept it. Now I guess she'll have to."

Steve spread his hands. "Maybe we should ask her what her magic formula is."

"I'm afraid it's a whole different situation."

He sighed. "I know it is. I was just—Alice, it's like being in a maze. You think you see a way out, and so you hurry around the corner, only to find you're in just as deep as you ever were."

This time it was she who reached out to him, touching her finger to his cheek then to his lips before taking her hand away. "Darling," she said, "the way out will come. It has to, and so it will. We have to be patient, that's all."

"So easy to say. So hard to do—"

Alice shook her head. "What's hard to do, Steven, is to walk away from you, but I can't stay any longer. I probably shouldn't have agreed to meet you here at all."

He frowned. "Did your mother kick up a fuss?"

"No. But she wasn't happy about it, and it puts a strain on things."

"I'm sorry," he said.

"Don't worry about it. I'm handling it."

She said that to reassure him, but the conflict with her mother about her relationship to Steven Frame was building. As far as Mary Matthews was concerned, there was no difference between Steven meeting Alice while he was still married to Rachel and his meeting Rachel while he had been married to Alice. Quarreling about it that same night, the climax came when her mother said, "If there's never been anything between Steven and Rachel except Jamie, he wouldn't still be living with her."

Enraged, Alice shot back, "He's not living with her. Not the way you mean."

"You have only his word for that."

Alice stared at her mother. "I don't have to stand and

181

listen to this." Going to the foyer closet for her coat, she stormed out of the house.

Things were never so bad after that, but shortly before Christmas, unable to bear the added strain her mother was putting on her, she told her parents she was moving to an apartment of her own. Her mother was further distressed to learn that Alice would be sharing the apartment with a former enemy—Steve's sister, Janice.

It was, Mary observed to Jim, a topsy-turvy world, and one she was finding it harder and harder to understand.

One evening in January John Randolph drove out to the big house in the country, Alice's erstwhile dream house, to speak to Rachel. He found her there alone.

Her greeting to him as she ushered him into the house was, "Now I see why Steve wanted me to stay home alone tonight."

Taking off his coat, John said, "Where is Steve?"

"As if you didn't know."

John hung his coat in the foyer closet and followed Rachel into the living room where a fire crackled in the fireplace. "If I knew, Rachel, I wouldn't have asked. I don't play games with my clients."

She shrugged. "He says he took Jamie to a basketball game."

They sat down, Rachel curling up on the sofa in front of the fireplace, John sitting in a nearby armchair. Putting down his briefcase he said, "I'm sorry things haven't worked out for you, Rachel."

"Oh, sure," she said. "You and all the rest of the Matthews family circle."

Ignoring that, John opened his briefcase. "I came out here to tell you Steve is filing for a divorce."

"On what grounds?" she snapped.

"Fraud. Steve thinks you were in collusion with your father in breaking up his marriage to Alice." John wasn't sure what he thought, but he'd been unable to come up with any other grounds for filing for a divorce, and what he was hoping was that Rachel, faced with the fraud charge, would want to file for the divorce herself out of pride. Then the burden of proof would shift to her.

If she was about to do that, she gave no sign of it. "What Steve thinks isn't true," she said. "I had nothing to do with what my father did."

"Steve doesn't agree."

She shrugged again. "So? It's his word against mine, and I'd say my word is at least as good as his."

John took a small notebook out of the briefcase. "We might have more than Steve's word, Rachel. We might bring your father here." After Steve's turndown of Gerald's request for help, Gerald had gone back to San Francisco.

Rachel stared at John in disbelief. "My father wouldn't come to Bay City to testify against me."

"We could force him to come. We could subpoena him."

Rachel still gave no sign of caving in, merely saying, "So force him. He's still not going to testify against me. He knows when he told me what he'd done—and it was months and months after he'd done it. So you're not going to prove anything."

Silence settled on the room, the only sounds the snap and crackle of the flaming logs. "Rachel," John said at last, "a contested divorce action is usually a messy, unpleasant affair. People can get hurt. Children especially."

Rachel turned to him. "So? I'm not the one who's making all this happen. Talk to the person who is."

"What I'm suggesting is that if you file for a divorce from Steve, it won't be contested."

"Is that what he sent you here to say?"

"No, not at all. Steve asked me to tell you he's filing for a divorce and on what grounds. The rest of it is my own suggestion. My recommendation."

Rachel stood up. "Well, you can keep your recommendation and your suggestion, because I'm not buying. I don't care how much of a fuss his divorce action kicks up. I can ride that out. And so can Jamie, if that's what you're thinking. Of course it may turn him against his father. He might not want to have anything more to do with his father afterward. But then that's not my doing either. It's Steve's." She watched the flames rise and fall, and then turned back to John. "And what happens when you aren't able to prove fraud? What then?"

John made a note. "If that were the case, the judge would have to rule against Steve."

"Meaning no divorce?"

"Right."

Rachel folded her arms across her chest. "Then you might as well save yourself all the paperwork and trouble because that's what there's going to be—no divorce. Steve won't be able to get one from me, and I'm certainly not going to file for one from him."

"Rachel—" John began.

She cut him off. "I don't want to hear anything more you have to say. I didn't marry Steve for his money, whatever you or anybody else thinks. I married him because I love him, and I am not going to hand him over to Alice, do you understand? Not now and not ever, and that's final."

And for the time being, at least, that was that.